IT'S COMPLICATED

A DIRTY LOVE NOVEL

R.L. KENDERSON

ISBN-13: 978-1-950918-25-6

Editor: Jovana Shirley, Unforeseen Editing, www.unforeseenediting.com
Cover Art by R.L. Kenderson, www.rlkenderson.com

PROLOGUE

Tiana Hall hadn't planned on flirting with her brother's groomsman. After all, it was a bit cliché for a bridesmaid to hook up with another member of the wedding party.

But there was something about Ty that was hard to resist. Maybe it was because she had a thing for older men. Maybe it was because she hadn't had sex in a long time. Maybe it was because she would end up having too much to drink at the reception. Or maybe it was because, sometimes, a woman simply needed a long fuck after a long night. Either way, Tiana had a feeling that before the evening ended, she was going to be coming all over Ty Morgan's dick.

Tiana, the groom's sister, moved into place at the end of the processional next to Ty, her brother's friend.

Her soon-to-be sister-in-law, Piper, was in the front with her mom. Piper's father had passed away, so her mother was giving her away. Then, it was Piper's cousin, Cindy, the maid of honor, who was walking down the aisle with Luke, the groom's best man and best friend.

"Are you ready for this?" Tiana asked Ty.

He sardonically scratched his dark chin. "I don't know. We only walked down the aisle three times last night. What if I accidentally steer right or left?" His deep brown eyes glistened with humor, and Tiana smiled.

She wouldn't have been able to resist returning his grin if she'd wanted to. Ty Morgan was one fine black man. Fine *older* black man. At twenty-four, Tiana always found men in their thirties sexier than guys her own age. Ty was around her brother, Nate's, age, maybe a little older, and Nate was nine years older than her.

"It's a good thing I'll be holding on to your arm," she told him. "I'll make sure you walk in a straight line," she teased him.

"Good." He looked into her eyes. "Maybe you can help me walk in a straight line after the wedding reception, too. I have a feeling your brother's going to fill me with drinks."

Tiana played it cool. "Does this mean you're not going to ditch me at the reception?" she asked casually.

"Of course not."

The music started playing in the chapel and the words, "All rise," could be heard through the double doors.

Ty leaned down closer to her ear. "You are my date after all, right? That's what walking down the aisle together means."

Tiana turned her head, and their faces were inches apart. She sucked in a breath and swallowed. "I don't think that's an official rule." She pointed to the couple in front of them. "Luke is married to someone else."

The corner of Ty's mouth lifted. "Then, let's make it our rule. You're my date tonight." He held out his arm as the doors to the chapel opened.

She slipped her hand in the crook of his elbow. "You've got yourself a deal."

The wedding was short and beautiful. Her brother looked especially handsome in his tux, and her new sister-in-law looked stunning in her wedding gown. No one could tell that she was five months pregnant even though the two of them weren't keeping it a secret.

They had just finished dinner, and the tables were being cleared away to make room for the dance. Tiana excused herself from the rest of the wedding party and headed for the bar. Piper was sweet, but Tiana didn't know her very well.

"White wine, please," Tiana told the bartender.

"You weren't trying to ditch me, were you?" a deep voice said from behind her.

She looked over her shoulder and tilted her head. "I thought you'd ditched me. You left the table and didn't come back."

"Never," Ty said. "I was waiting for you to finish."

"Waiting for me to finish, huh?" She met his dark eyes and licked her bottom lip. "What a gentleman."

Tiana heard the clink of her glass hitting the bar, so she turned her back to Ty to grab it.

"Whiskey, neat," he said to the bartender. Then, she felt him move closer, and his breath fanned over her ear. "If you play your cards right, you'll find out how many times I let you finish before me."

Tiana's breath got stuck in her throat as the area between her legs practically caught on fire. She composed herself and turned around.

"If *you* play *your* cards right, maybe, just maybe, I'll be the one letting *you* find out if you can get me to finish before you." She took a sip of her wine, gave him a wink, and walked away.

"Challenge accepted," she heard him say behind her.

Tiana grinned all the way to the dance floor.

CHAPTER ONE

THREE MONTHS LATER

Ty Morgan came around the corner of his block and slowed from a jog to a walk as he wiped his brow on the shoulder of his tank.

He looked down at his watch. It was just after eight on a Saturday, and he had already done some chores around his house and gone for a run. If he kept this up, he wouldn't have anything to do in the afternoon.

As he neared his house, he saw that someone was sitting on his front steps. He couldn't make out who it was because he was too far away, so he racked his brain to see if he'd made plans with someone and forgotten about them.

Nothing came to mind, so he picked up his pace again. The first thing he noticed was that it was a woman. He knew he didn't have plans with a woman. He hadn't gone on a date for at least a month. His interest got the best of him, and he broke out into a run.

But when her face finally came into focus, he made a full stop.

What the hell is Tiana Hall doing at my house?

He hadn't seen Nate's sister for months. Not since Nate and Piper's wedding. At first, he'd been upset to wake up alone after a night of phenomenal sex. But after a week, he'd come to the conclusion it was for the best.

If Nate knew that Ty had slept with his sister, there was a strong chance Nate would castrate him. No, Nate would *definitely* cut off Ty's balls. Nate sometimes talked about Tiana like she was a kid. He refused to see that his little sister was a woman now.

Ty sucked in a deep breath and walked toward his house and Tiana. As he went, he thought through all the things she could possibly be there for.

She had on jeans and a T-shirt. Her corkscrew curls were up, and she didn't have on makeup, yet she still looked gorgeous. Her full lips were kissable, and the smooth tawny skin on her neck brought back memories of his mouth being there. It wasn't a surprise that Nate was protective of her.

She also looked anxious, her beautiful amber eyes hesitant, so he smiled at her.

"Hey."

"Sorry to drop in on you like this. I thought about calling you, but I was afraid I'd chicken out."

"How did you know where I lived?" he asked.

"I called my new sister-in-law and asked her. I told her I needed help with my laptop because it had a virus."

Ty raised his eyebrows. "Oh?" Weird that she hadn't asked Nate. But then again, Nate would have probably questioned her too much. Ty reminded himself about the ball removal his friend would take upon himself to do if he found out what had happened between him and Tiana. "That was probably a good idea."

"Yeah," she said, wringing her hands together.

She had his curiosity piqued now. Was she going to ask him out? It was cute that she was nervous. He'd already lectured himself on not messing around with Nate's sister again, but if she asked him out, he decided he'd say yes.

Because seeing Tiana up close brought him back to the wedding. They'd flirted for two nights straight. First, on the rehearsal night and then the wedding night.

By the time the dance had been over, the two of them had been so full of sexual tension, they'd attacked each other just through the door of his hotel room. They hadn't even made it to the bed before he had his mouth on her pussy. She'd tasted so sweet.

And just like that, he was hard.

And in gym shorts.

Shit.

"Why don't you come inside?" he said now to Tiana. He turned around, so he could use his garage code and go into the house that way. It also gave him a chance to adjust himself as best he could.

"Thank you," she said, following behind him.

He opened his garage and showed her inside his home. "Have a seat anywhere. I just need to go and get changed real quick."

Tiana took a step toward him and held up her hands. "No. Please, don't."

His brow furrowed. "Okay."

She laughed uncertainly. "If I don't come out and say it, there's a chance I might just leave. I used up all my willpower, waiting for you on the front step."

She was adorable. He didn't normally go for someone so young, but she was hard to resist. Beautiful and smart. And a firecracker in bed. He'd forgotten how wild women in their twenties could be between the sheets.

Ty decided to help her out. He stepped closer to her. "Hey. Don't be nervous. I know it's been a while since we last saw each other, but I'd love to go out with you."

She leaned back as her eyes widened in a *you be crazy* look. "No, Ty, I didn't come here to ask you out."

"Oh," he said, surprised and a little disappointed. He hadn't realized how much he'd been looking forward to hanging out with her again. It was his turn to laugh awkwardly. "Okay then. What's going on?"

She exhaled a big breath. She was anxious again, and Ty's heart began to beat faster. Whatever it was, it wasn't good.

Oh shit. She is—

"I'm pregnant."

The good thing was that he didn't have to worry about his nuts anymore because he wouldn't need his balls if he was dead. Nate was going to fucking kill him.

CHAPTER TWO

Ty's chest started to hurt. "I think I need to sit down."

"I think you might also need to breathe."

He sucked in a breath, and the pain behind his sternum eased. He honestly had no idea what to say to Tiana's news. Emotions bombarded him. Everything from panic to being excited to a fierce heartache.

"Would you like to come sit down?" he asked her, taking a few minutes to compose himself.

"Actually, do you have anything to eat? I apologize. I just left my house without breakfast, and I'm now realizing that wasn't a good idea."

"Yes," he said, leading her into the kitchen. "Would you like some coffee?"

She set her purse on the counter and shook her head. "No. Water is fine. Do you have any saltines?"

"I'll check." He pointed to his row of stools. "Please sit."

He opened his pantry and moved some boxes around. "Sorry. I have Ritz Crackers, if that works?"

"Sure," she said with a smile as she took a seat.

Ty carried the box over to the counter where she was sitting. "So, are you sure—"

Tiana's eyes narrowed. "Yes, I'm sure it's yours. You're the only guy I've been with in the last five months, which is probably more than I can say for you."

Ty held his hands up in surrender. "Whoa, whoa, whoa. I wasn't going to ask that. I was going to ask if you were sure you were pregnant. We used condoms."

She chuckled awkwardly. "Oh. Uh...sorry." She rolled her eyes. "Hormones."

He laughed. "I guess there's my answer."

"Along with four at-home pregnancy tests, two missed periods, and a blood test at my doctor's office. And condoms aren't a hundred percent effective, you know."

Ty winced. "Right. Of course." His eyes changed to sympathetic. "I'm sorry."

Tiana tilted her head. "For what?"

"That you had to go through all that alone."

She shrugged. "It's not a big deal."

He couldn't quite tell if she meant it or if she was trying to convince herself.

"So, how far along are you?"

"Almost twelve weeks."

Ty stared at her belly, studying it. He knew the baby would be too small to cause Tiana to show, but he wished he could see the proof. Not because he didn't believe her, but because he wanted to be able to see where his child grew.

"Ty?"

He looked up to Tiana's face. "Yeah?"

"Are you okay?"

The answer was no, but she didn't need to know about his past. She was here about her future.

"Yes." He smiled and shook his head. "I was thinking about what your brother is going to do to me when he finds out." It was partly the truth. He had been thinking about it earlier.

"I haven't decided if I'm going to keep it yet."

Ty's chest was feeling tight again. "If you feel as if you're not ready, I would be more than willing to take full responsibility," he offered. "I have a good job. And I love kids," he added.

Tiana's jaw clenched. "You misunderstand. I'm not sure if I'm going to have this baby at all. I was finally ready to go to grad school in the fall. I don't have time to be pregnant, have a baby, and go on maternity leave."

Now, it felt as if all the air had been sucked out of Ty's lungs. He suddenly felt like he was seventeen again. This couldn't be happening.

"Can't you put off grad school until the baby is born?"

Tiana raised her brow and straightened her spine. "Oh. I see. You want me to stay home, barefoot and pregnant, while you go off to work. Having your child is more important than my career." She leaned toward him. "I already waited two years to go back to school until I saved up some money. And no man is going to tell me what to do." She slammed down the crackers that had been in her hand. She jumped off the stool and grabbed her purse.

"Wait."

"What?" she asked, her voice filled with anger.

"I'm not saying I want you to stay home while I go to work."

"Then, what are you trying to say?"

There was no way he could say what he wanted in a good way. "I don't know. But I don't want you to have an abortion."

"Yeah? The last time I checked, it was a woman's right to choose. At least, in the state of Minnesota it is. And you don't have a say."

She waited for him to say something, but he stood silent.

"That's what I thought," Tiana said and headed to the door.

Ty collapsed on the stool she had just vacated and put his head on the counter. He'd really fucked up that conversation. He hadn't meant to make it sound like he was trying to force her to do anything.

He'd panicked. He was reliving the worst time in his life. He could still see Robin's face when she'd told him.

Ty whipped his head up. No way. He wasn't going back there.

That was a long time ago. He was older and wiser. He needed to find Tiana and apologize. He needed to let her know he would be with her, no matter what she decided.

But first, he needed to find a way to get ahold of her. He couldn't call Nate. But he thought he remembered her saying something about her new sister-in-law...

Ty pulled his phone from his pocket and found Piper's number.

"Hello?"

"Hey, Piper. It's Ty."

"Yes?"

"Can you give me Tiana's address?" He didn't want to have this conversation over the phone.

"Why?"

He tried to remember what Tiana had said she told Piper. "Uh...her computer. She brought it over for me to fix, but she left before I could get some of the info I need from her."

"Uh-huh. And why can't I give you her phone number instead?"

He couldn't be sure, but it sounded like Piper was teasing him.

"Hey, I'll take that, too. But it would save me time if I could go to her house now. I'm on my way to"—*Shit. Think, Ty. Think.* He scanned the room until he saw a small cardboard box—"the post office. And you know how they close early on Saturdays."

"Hmm..."

"Please, Piper."

She laughed. "Okay. But it'll cost you."

"I have to pay you to give me Tiana's information?"

She laughed again. "No. It'll cost you for me to keep this quiet from my husband."

CHAPTER THREE

Tiana sighed as she drove home from her favorite bakery. Today had not gone the way she'd planned it.

Although she really didn't know what she had expected—or even wanted—from Ty. But she did know she hadn't wanted to fight with him.

She shoved the last bite of her cookie in her mouth and wiped her hand on the napkin in her lap. As she chewed, she contemplated what her next step should be.

She knew she needed to talk to Ty again, but he probably didn't want to see her after the way she'd yelled at him.

She blamed her hormones.

She blamed her family more.

As she was the youngest and a female, her father and brother had always been protective of her, and there were times when they still didn't treat her as an adult. She was twenty-four fricking years old, and they treated her like she was fourteen.

So, when Ty had started giving her his opinion on what she should do, she'd sort of lost it. She was tired of people thinking they knew what was best for her.

When Tiana reached home, she pulled into the driveway. The house was a small three-bedroom that her roommate owned. Tiana and Shannon worked with one another together, and even though they weren't close, Tiana had jumped at the chance to move in with Shannon. Shannon had someone to help with the mortgage, and Tiana got to save more money than she would if she were living on her own.

It was actually nice that the two of them weren't close. They both kept their space clean, and they stayed out of each other's way. There was no forced time they had to spend with one another just because they shared a roof. But they did watch the occasional TV show together.

Of course, now, all that was going to change once she had the baby.

She didn't want to think about it, so she shoved the panic down as she grabbed her bag of goodies and exited her car. As she walked toward the front door, there was movement, and Tiana realized someone was sitting there.

"Hello?" she called out as she stopped in her tracks.

The figure stood, and she was surprised to see it was Ty.

"Hey," he said, his deep brown eyes hesitant.

"Hey," she said back. "I wasn't expecting to see you so soon."

He ran his hand over his cropped dark hair. "I came to apologize."

When she'd gone to his house to tell him about the baby, she hadn't planned on feeling anything. But seeing him again, she'd been reminded of their night together. She'd planned on it being a one-time thing, but then he'd had to show up all sexy from working out, sporting facial hair that had probably been a five o'clock shadow the night before.

It was clear to her that she was still attracted to him, and having a baby together was going to be more difficult than she had previously thought. This added to her frustration, but it wasn't Ty's fault she felt that way.

Tiana moved forward. "That's sweet of you. But I think I need to apologize, too. I had no right to jump down your throat." When she reached him, she asked, "Why are you waiting outside? Is my roommate not home?"

"She's home. I decided to wait out here for you."

"Is this payback for me waiting on your front steps?"

Ty looked surprised. "What? No. I thought it was better out here. I didn't want your roommate to start asking questions that I don't have the answers for."

"That was a joke. But a good idea." Tiana sat down on the cement steps, and Ty followed.

He turned to her. "I'm sorry I tried to make your decision for you. I..." He rubbed a hand over his face. "I..."

She put a hand on his knee but immediately removed it. She wasn't sure if that was appropriate. "It's okay. You don't have to say any more."

"No, it's not that. I want to. It's just hard."

"We can talk about it later. Circle back if you want."

"I've been in a similar situation before," he blurted out.

Tiana nodded slowly. "Okay. We can talk about it now then."

Ty tried to smile, but she could tell his mind was on something else.

"In high school, my girlfriend got pregnant. We were both seventeen and about to start our senior year. I didn't care. I was so excited. I had always wanted to be a dad. But her parents were livid, and without even a conversation, they hauled her off and made her get an abortion."

Tiana winced. "Oh, Ty."

He stared off into space. "She'd be seventeen now. The baby." He chuckled sadly. "Kind of ironic."

"It was a little girl?"

He shrugged. "I don't know. My ex wasn't far enough along. I always pictured her being a girl though."

"I'm sorry."

He looked at her. "It's not your fault. I just...I just wanted you to know where I was coming from. I agree one hundred and ten percent that the decision is up to you and that it's your body and your right. But I also think a woman can't make a full decision until she knows how the father feels if she's having any doubts."

Tiana nodded. "You are right. That's why I came to your house after all."

"So, what are you going back to school for?"

Tiana's eyes went wide. She hadn't expected the subject change. "A master's in accounting. I'll have more opportunities as a CPA, which requires a fifth year of school." She wished she had gone all the way when she started college, but she had wanted to save some money after graduation.

"That's right. I think I knew that about you." He smiled to himself.

"What?"

"I should probably know what my baby mama does for a living."

Tiana wrinkled her nose. "Ugh...don't call me that."

Ty laughed. "Now, it's my turn to joke. But, yeah, I should probably know what you do since we had sex and made a baby." He laughed again. "Wow. That sounds weird. We made a baby." He shook his head as if it were the craziest thing he'd ever heard.

But she had to agree. It wasn't something she'd thought she'd hear him say.

Tiana had always planned to finish school, fall in love, get married, and then have a baby. Her plans never seemed to work out.

"So, about that baby," she said.

Ty's face turned serious. "I will support you in whatever you do." He met her eyes. "If you want to keep the baby, I will pay child support, and I will do whatever you need me to do to help you get through school. If you want to give the baby up for adoption, I will help you find the perfect adoptive parents. But I also want you to know that I would be more than willing to take full custody and raise the child as a single father. I would actually love the chance to be a dad. And I wouldn't ask anything of you in return." He closed his eyes, took a breath in and out, and opened them again. "And if you want to go to the clinic, I will drive you and hold your hand. If that's what you want. Or I can sit in the waiting room if you'd rather be alone."

Tiana smiled. "Thank you." She tilted her head. "Would

you be okay if I told you I wasn't sure yet what I wanted to do? That I'm still thinking about it?"

"Of course. It's a big decision." Ty smiled and stood. "I'd better get going then. I have to pick up some chocolate, potato chips, and ice cream."

"What for?"

"It's my payment to Piper for giving me your address. And I'd better deliver before Nate gets home, or he's going to wonder why I'm bringing his pregnant wife food."

Tiana chuckled.

"What did you have to do to get my address?"

She shrugged and stood up. "Nothing. I'm the sister-in-law, remember?"

"Yeah. Figures." His words sounded bitter, but he was smiling.

"Thanks for coming by," she said.

"Thanks for letting me." Ty smiled and walked away.

"Ty?"

He stopped and turned around. "Yeah?"

"I have a doctor's appointment on Wednesday. Would you like to come with me?"

He beamed. "I'd love to." He rattled off his phone number. "Send me the deets. I'll be there."

She pulled her phone from her purse and put his number in her Contacts. "I'll send it as soon as I get inside."

Tiana hadn't been sure about inviting him, but seeing the grin on his face, she knew she'd made the right decision.

CHAPTER FOUR

Nate: Want to hit up the Chinese place for lunch?

Ty stared down at his message, trying to think of a good reply. It was Wednesday, and he was using the majority of his lunch break to go to the doctor with Tiana. Ty had a feeling that Nate wouldn't respond well to that.

Before Ty could reply, there was a knock at his cubicle. He swung his chair around to see the last person he wanted to face.

"Hey." Nate leaned forward, his bald head catching the light above his computer, and looked at the phone in Ty's hand. "Oh, so you did get my text."

Ty tried to smile. "Yeah. I was just about to text you back. I can't go today. I have a doctor's appointment." Caught on the spot, Ty hadn't known what else to say. He supposed it was the truth. It just wasn't his doctor's appointment.

Nate frowned. "You okay?"

"What?" Ty waved his hand in front of him. "Yeah. Routine. Nothing to worry about."

Now, that was a lie.

Nate narrowed his eyes. "Are you sure you're not just avoiding me? I feel like I've hardly seen you all week."

"It's the truth."

"That you've been avoiding me?"

"No, dumbass, that I'm going to the clinic today." Ty looked away, setting his phone on his desk. "And I haven't been avoiding you."

Lie, lie, lie.

Before Nate could say anything else, Ty added, "I just have a lot on my mind."

Nate sat on the edge of Ty's desk. "Everything okay?"

"Yeah, yeah."

Nate raised an eyebrow.

Maybe it wouldn't hurt to talk to someone about it. Ty didn't need to mention any names. And Nate had found himself in a similar position. He'd gotten his wife pregnant before they got married.

Ty sighed. "Okay, but this stays between the two of us, all right?"

Nate nodded.

"A girl—woman—I had a one-night stand with a while ago came to me and told me she was pregnant."

Nate whistled. "You dog." He straightened. "Please tell me it's not Vanessa or Simone."

Ty laughed.

Vanessa had been one of Nate's regulars before he started

dating Piper. Ty'd had sex with her a couple of times, but that had been some time ago. And Simone was one of Piper's friends. The two of them had run into each other one night and gone home together. Ty was beginning to think he really was a dog.

"No, man, it's not either of them."

"That's good. Piper would be mad if you knocked up her friend."

Ty winced. *Probably not as mad as you'll be when you find out it's your sister.*

"Who is it?" Nate asked.

"No one you know." The lies were just rolling off his tongue now.

"What are you going to do?"

Ty shrugged. "Nothing. It's not up to me. It's up to her, and she doesn't know what she wants to do yet."

"What do you want?"

Nate knew a little bit of Ty's history with his high school girlfriend.

"I want her to keep the baby." He met Nate's eyes. "I really don't know if I can lose another one again."

Nate squeezed Ty's shoulder. "That's rough."

"Yeah. I'm trying not to think too hard about it."

"Good idea. Don't worry about it until you have to."

The corner of Ty's mouth lifted. "Thanks, man."

That's easier said than done.

CHAPTER FIVE

Tiana paced back and forth in front of the clinic. Her appointment was in five minutes, and Ty still hadn't shown up.

She checked her phone again. He also hadn't responded to her text message when she asked him if he was still coming.

Her heart sank. She had been prepared to do all the pregnancy stuff alone, but after talking to Ty and seeing his enthusiasm, she'd realized how much her hopes had lifted because she would have someone to go through the experience with.

She should have known he was all talk and that he wouldn't actually want anything to do with the baby.

She was such a sucker. He'd really had her going with the ex-girlfriend story. She had to wonder if any of it was true.

She turned to go into the building when she heard the screeching of tires. She looked to the road as a car sped into the parking lot and came to a stop in the nearest open parking spot.

The driver's door flung open, and Tiana heard her name being called.

Ty jumped out and waved his arm. "I'm here. Wait for me."

Tiana tried to stop the grin from spreading across her face but didn't succeed.

Ty jogged over to her, looking very fine in his black dress pants and light-blue button-down shirt. "I'm sorry I'm late. I had a stupid meeting that ran over, and I didn't think it was in good form for me to tell him to hurry up when he was already letting me take a long lunch break." He opened the door for Tiana.

She chuckled and walked into the building. "That's probably a good idea. I was actually a little late, too. But my excuse isn't as good. I lost track of time."

"Hey, it happens." Ty rubbed his chin as the two of them got in line to check in. "So, your brother came to me today and asked why I wouldn't go to lunch with him."

Tiana's eyes widened. "What did you say?"

"I told him I had to go to the doctor. I neglected to tell him that it wasn't my appointment and what it was for."

"Didn't he ask?"

"Yeah. I told him it was something routine." He sighed. "I did the smart thing, right?"

She put her hand on his arm. "Yes. I'm barely into my second trimester. If I keep the baby, I do not want to tell everyone yet." If she could go without telling anyone ever, that would be even better. Her family wasn't going to be happy.

"Thank God. I'm not sure what Nate will do to me when he finds out."

Tiana winced. "Yeah. You're going to be on his shit list."

"Thanks," Ty said sarcastically.

She shrugged. "I don't want to lie to you."

"In this instance, I would have been okay with it."

The nurse took Tiana and Ty back to the exam room. They asked her a million and one questions, and then she sent Ty out while the doctor did her pap smear and physical exam. Just because they'd had sex once didn't mean she wanted him in the room while she lay naked under a sheet.

"Would you like Ty to come back in before we listen to the heartbeat?" the doctor asked.

"Yes, please."

"Okay. Go ahead and get dressed, and I'll bring him back in." She washed her hands and grabbed her paperwork. "And don't worry. The next few appointments will be less invasive. We won't have to kick dad out of the room every time."

"Thanks," Tiana said.

As soon as the doctor closed the door behind her, Tiana jumped down and put her clothes on as quickly as she could. The staff gave her plenty of time to dress, but she was always afraid they'd walk in when she was half-naked.

Ty and the doctor returned after a few minutes.

"Go ahead and lie down and pull your shirt up a bit, and

we'll see if we can hear the heartbeat," the doctor said with a smile.

Tiana did as she had been asked, and the doctor squirted a blob of cold gel on her bare belly. The doctor took a little white probe and placed it on her stomach.

Tiana wasn't sure if she'd hear the baby's heartbeat over the pounding of her own, and she held her breath in anticipation.

The doctor moved her hand around several times as the machine made static noises and frowned.

"What's wrong?" Ty asked.

Tiana looked at the doctor and then at Ty.

"I'm sure it's nothing, but I'd like to send you for an ultrasound. I'm having trouble hearing the heartbeat." The doctor wiped the gel off of Tiana's belly. "I'll go make some calls to see if I can get you in right away. If I can't, what time works for you?"

"I'm off today," Tiana said. She heard Ty shift beside her. "But Ty has to go back to work."

"Don't worry about me," Ty said. "You get Tiana in as soon as possible."

"I will be right back," the doctor said left the room, gently shutting the door.

The silence in the room felt like the air was being sucked out. She shouldn't have invited Ty to come to her first appointment. She should have made sure that the baby was okay before she even told him about the pregnancy. He was probably upset that she'd dragged him into the whole situation.

"I'm sorry."

Ty swung around from where he'd been pacing back and forth. "For what?"

"I should have come to the doctor and checked out before I—"

The door to the exam room opened, and the doctor walked in. "You're in luck. They can get you in for an ultrasound in about twenty minutes. The nurse will be here with your paperwork and directions on where to go."

"I'm here," the nurse said, coming up behind the doctor. She handed Tiana her paperwork. "You have to walk down to radiology—it's on the hospital side of the building; right now, you're on the clinic side—and check in at the front desk. When you're finished, come back here."

Tiana lay down on her second exam table of the day, and gel was squirted on her bare abdomen.

The walk down to radiology had been filled with more silence between her and Ty, minus his call to work that he'd be a little later than he'd previously planned. It was obvious that neither of them knew what to say to each other.

And right now, Tiana had never felt so scared or alone. Not even the day she'd taken the pregnancy tests.

She looked over at Ty standing next to her right before the sonographer was about to put the probe down on her belly and reveal whether or not their baby had a heartbeat.

Please look at me. Tiana didn't know why, but it was what she wanted most at that moment.

Ty looked down at her with concern in his eyes and a

reassuring smile on his face. Or at least, he attempted to give her one.

He lifted his arm but started to drop it, and she reached out and grabbed his hand. He supportively squeezed her fingers just as the probe landed on her stomach.

A tiny flicker of a beating heart showed up on the screen in front of them, and Tiana burst into tears.

CHAPTER SIX

N ot knowing what else to do, Ty gripped Tiana's hand as she cried.

The ultrasound technologist looked at Tiana with concern. "Are you okay? We can stop if you need to."

Tiana shook her head and sniffled. "No. I'm okay." She sniffled again.

The tech pointed behind Ty. "There're some tissues if you'd like to hand them to her."

Grateful for something else to do, he picked up the whole box and held it out for Tiana to grab as many as she wanted.

She smiled gratefully at him and pulled a couple out.

"Are you okay?" he asked. "Really?"

She nodded. "Yes. We'll talk about it later."

Her words concerned him. He'd been so excited to see a heartbeat flicker on the monitor, but he wasn't sure if Tiana was crying because she was happy or because she'd been hoping nature had taken care of the pregnancy and she wouldn't have to make any decisions now.

He tried not to think about any of it and simply concentrated on seeing their baby up on the screen, but the gnawing feeling in his gut was hard to ignore.

When the exam was over, the ultrasound tech cleaned the gel off Tiana's stomach and handed her some pictures she'd printed off.

The two of them left the room and walked through the hospital and then the clinic in silence again. Ty didn't know what to say to her, and she seemed lost in her own thoughts.

Outside the doors, there was a bench.

"Should we sit for a minute?" he asked.

"That'd be nice."

They sat, and Ty asked, "Do you mind if I look at the pics?"

"Oh." Tiana laughed. "Yes." She laughed again. "I mean, no." She shoved them at him. "Here you go. Just take them."

Ty flipped through the images, in awe of what was on there. Tiana wasn't very far along, but the baby already had arms and legs and a little spine, too.

"These are amazing."

"They are," she agreed.

"Do you mind if I keep one or two? I'll let you decide which ones you'd like me to have."

"You can have them all."

Dread filled Ty. There could only be one reason she didn't want the photos. She wasn't going to keep the pregnancy.

He didn't want to say anything wrong, so he took a breath before he spoke, "Thank you. I...I never got any images from the first baby, so it's nice that I'll have something to keep and look at when I think of the little guy."

Tiana leaned back and furrowed her brow. She looked at Ty like he'd grown an extra limb.

"What?" he asked.

"I'm keeping the baby, you fool."

A grin broke out across his face. "Really?" He was so happy; he didn't even care that she'd called him a fool.

Tiana smiled at him. "Yes. I realized how scared I was that there wouldn't be a heartbeat. And when I saw it flicker, the relief that rushed through me told me all I needed to know. I want this baby."

"For real?"

She laughed. "Yes. For real."

"Then, why don't you want any of the pictures?"

Tiana frowned and reached into her purse. "Because she gave me a whole CD with them on there. I can print some later if I want."

Ty leaned back on the bench and looked up to the sky. "I'm so..."

"Happy?" she offered.

He met her eyes. "Yes."

"Me, too."

"What about school?"

She shrugged, and her smile fell. "I don't know. I guess I was trying not to think about that."

"I will do whatever it is you need me to do to help." He picked up her hand. "I know you're the one pregnant, but we are in this together. Don't ever hesitate to ask me for anything."

She lifted her brow. "Even if I'm craving ice cream and pickles at two in the morning on a work night?"

"I'll do it."

She looked at him with doubt on her face. "You're going to get out of bed, drive to the store, and then come all the way to my house, just to bring me food?"

"If that's what you want."

"Mmhmm. We'll see about that."

Ty laughed. "I guess I'll have to prove myself."

"I guess you will." She smiled, pulled her hand from his, and pointed to the building. "I'd better go. I have to go back to the doctor."

Ty frowned. "Oh. That's right. Do you want me to go with you?"

"No. I'm sure she'll talk to me about the ultrasound results. You need to get back to work."

"Will you let me know if there's anything important I missed?"

"Yes." She stood up and shooed him toward the parking lot. "Now, get back to work. I have child support to collect."

Ty stood and frowned. "Oh, yeah. How do we go about doing that?"

Tiana rolled her eyes and laughed. "I was joking. I'm not asking you for anything."

"But I want to."

"We'll worry about that later. We have quite a few months left to figure things out."

Ty was a planner and didn't like waiting. "Okay. But I'm going to bug you about it soon."

"Warning received."

"It wasn't a warning."

Tiana put a hand on his chest. "Ty. Relax. I was kidding. This partnership is never going to work if you can't take a joke."

He forced himself to smile. "I can. I promise. I'm only worried."

"Well, stop. We got good news today. Let's talk about the future later. Okay?"

He nodded. "Okay. Dinner this weekend?"

She thought about it. "Sure. How about Saturday?" Friday was dinner with her family.

"Works for me," he said, his smile genuine now.

"Saturday it is. Now, seriously, go to work before you get fired. That's not going to do us any good."

He pretended to salute her. "Yes, ma'am."

"Oh, so you can joke."

"Yes, ma'am."

"You think you're funny, but you keep doing it, and I'm going to start liking it."

He laughed and kissed her on the cheek. "I'll see you on Saturday, Tiana."

As he walked away, he spun around to wave good-bye. Tiana had her hand on her cheek and a smile on her lips.

CHAPTER SEVEN

"I'm here," Tiana called out as the front door to her parents' house closed behind her.

Piper appeared from around the corner. "You and I need to talk."

"Oh?" Tiana played dumb. "What about?" she asked as she tried to walk past her sister-in-law, but Piper was using her big belly to block the hallway.

Piper lowered her voice. "Why did I give your address to Ty, and why did you need his?"

Tiana looked away. "I told you, my computer." She wasn't the best liar, and she knew Piper would see it all over her face if they made eye contact.

"Tiana, I need you to look at me."

She started to slowly turn her head when her brother walked up behind his wife.

"Hey, you two. What are you doing?"

"Talking," Tiana said.

Nate wrapped his arms around Piper and kissed her on

the neck as he rubbed his hands on her bulging stomach. "That sounds like fun," he said as he nuzzled his wife.

Tiana wrinkled her nose and made a gagging noise. "Gross."

Nate stood up straight. "Hey," he protested.

"I'd tell you to get a room, but it's apparent you already have," Tiana said, looking at Piper's belly.

"I shouldn't have to take this abuse from you," her brother said with narrowed eyes.

Tiana lifted her hands and shrugged. "That's what little sisters are for." She managed to squeeze by the two lovebirds.

"You just wait until you're pregnant and all lovey-dovey with your husband. I'm going to give you so much shit."

It was a good thing her back was to her brother because she was sure he'd know something was up if he saw her face. She pulled herself together and spun on her heel. "That will never happen," she said sweetly. She turned back around and headed for the kitchen.

At least, it wasn't going to happen with this pregnancy because she didn't have a husband. She didn't even have a boyfriend. Hell, she wasn't even dating someone.

"Thanks, Nate," she muttered under her breath. Nothing like being reminded how alone she was.

Tiana and her family were just finishing up dinner when her mom asked for the third time that night, "Are you sure you don't want any wine?"

"Mom, I already told you no."

Piper suspiciously narrowed her green eyes at Tiana. Tiana ignored her sister-in-law.

"I'll have a bit more, Tricia," Nate said, and her mom poured him a drink.

Nate was technically Tiana's half-brother because his mom had died when he was very little. But she never thought of him as half even if he looked a little different from the rest of the family.

Nate's mom was half-Caucasian and half-Mexican while their dad was half-black and half-white, so his skin was lighter than the rest of them.

Her dad chuckled. "I remember you couldn't wait to drink at the table with us. You always complained that it wasn't fair that Nate got to drink and you couldn't."

Tiana held up her finger. "Okay, first of all, I was in high school. I didn't think anything was fair back then. And two, I just don't feel like drinking tonight. I don't know what I'm doing after or how far I'll have to drive."

She had to bite her tongue not to say any more because she knew that if she got too defensive, they might suspect something was up. It was a good thing her parents weren't big drinkers. She didn't know how long she could dodge no alcohol.

She might need to buy her parents a plant to pour her drinks into.

Actually...

That gave her an idea.

"You know what? I think I will have a little," she said.

Her mom smiled as she poured her half a glass. Out of

the corner of her eye, Piper looked confused, and Nate was looking at his phone.

"Ty has been evading me all week, and now, he says he has plans tomorrow night," Nate said.

Tiana brought her glass to her lips and pretended to take a sip. "I'll help with the dishes," she said as she stood. She grabbed her wineglass and her plate.

As she carried them to the kitchen, she heard Piper say, "That's kind of weird. But can't you hang out with Luke or someone else?"

"Luke doesn't want to do anything now that he has a baby," Nate complained.

"That's going to be you soon," Piper pointed out.

"I know. That's why I want to go out now."

Tiana chuckled to herself. Her brother did have a point.

She took a quick glance over her shoulder to make sure no one had followed her and poured her wine in the sink. She turned on the water and rinsed her plate until all the alcohol was down the drain.

Just as she was loading her dishes into the dishwasher, her phone buzzed.

> Ty: How is dinner with the family going?

> Tiana: How did you know I was having dinner with my family?

> Ty: Nate told me. He wants me to hang tomorrow night. I had to make something up. If I keep this up, he's going to think something's going on.

Tiana: He already does. He told Piper you've been avoiding him all week.

Ty: Shit. Unfortunately, he's not wrong.

Ty: I don't know how to look at him. I know he's not going to be happy once he finds out about what we did.

Tiana: Which part? The part where you were inside me or the part where you put your baby in me?

Tiana waited, but there was no response. Maybe she'd been a bit too forward in her messaging, but right now, Ty was the one she could be completely truthful with. No hiding anything. She might have been a little too free with her thoughts.

Tiana: You still there?

Ty: Yes.

Tiana: What happened to you?

Ty: Truth?

Tiana: Always.

Ty: I had to look away from your words before I took myself in my hand and got myself off.

Tiana licked her lips. She hadn't meant to go sexual, but now that he'd said that, she pictured the way he had picked her up in his hotel room and slid her down over his dick.

She closed her eyes and took a deep breath. Ty was not a small man, and he had filled every inch of her. No wonder she had gotten pregnant. She was amazed the condom hadn't broken.

She lifted her phone.

> Tiana: I'm surprised you don't have someone you can call up to fuck.

Tiana knew her brother had been like that before Piper even though he'd tried to hide it from her. It wouldn't surprise her to know Ty was the same. Although the idea of it made her a little uncomfortable.

> Ty: Baby, right now, I'm only thinking about you.

Wow. She didn't even know what to say back.

> Ty: Did I scare you away?

> Tiana: No. I just wasn't expecting it.

> Ty: Expecting what?

> Tiana: That you would be thinking about me.

> Ty: If you think that, then maybe you forgot about being in my room the night of the wedding because you know we had a good time. A real good time.

> Tiana: I remember.

> Ty: Then, maybe you need a refresher course on how good it really was.

CHAPTER EIGHT

Tiana slung her purse over her shoulder and grabbed her keys from the front pocket. She had to meet Ty in a half hour for dinner, and she was excited to see him again. So much so that it had taken her forty-five minutes to pick out an outfit.

"Hey, Tiana?" Shannon yelled from the kitchen just as Tiana reached the front door.

She turned around to see what her roommate wanted.

"Yes?" Tiana asked, entering the room.

Shannon and her boyfriend, Hank, were standing in there, looking worried. Shannon's pale skin was flushed, and Hank wouldn't look her in the eye.

Something was up.

"Can this wait? I'm supposed to meet a friend for dinner."

"I'll be quick," Shannon said.

"Okay." Tiana waited, but her roommate didn't say

anything at first. "Look, I need to get going. Can you please tell me what's wrong?"

Shannon looked at Hank and then Tiana. "Hank is moving in."

"That's it?" That wasn't a big deal. Hank was around all the time anyway. "As long as he doesn't eat my food, I'm fine with it," she joked to let the couple know she was okay with the new arrangement.

Shannon looked like she was about to throw up instead of feeling relieved. "That's not it." She cringed. "I'm sorry, but Hank and I want to live here alone. Just the two of us."

"Oh. I see." Tiana had been prepared to move out because of the baby, but she'd thought she would have a few months to do so. This was something she didn't need right now. "How much time do I have? Can you give me a couple of weeks at least?"

"Oh, no." Shannon waved her hands back and forth. "You don't have to move out that soon."

That was a relief.

"My lease isn't up for another two months," Hank said.

Okay, so two months wasn't as good as six, but she could manage. Hopefully.

"Okay. Two months. Got it."

"You're not mad, are you?" Shannon asked.

"No." *Just worried and scared but not mad.* "It's your house after all." She looked at the clock on the oven. "I'd better go though, or I'm going to be late."

"Okay. Have fun," Shannon said.

Tiana tried to smile. "Thanks." She had no desire to go

out to eat now. "I'll try." But suddenly, she'd rather start apartment-hunting.

Ty quickly jogged from his car to the door of the restaurant. He was running late to meet Tiana. Again. Thankfully, he was only five minutes behind schedule.

He pulled open the door and was relieved to see her still sitting on the bench, waiting for a table. He would have felt like shit if she'd been sitting at a table by herself.

She looked up from her phone and smiled, but it didn't light up her face the way it normally did.

What the hell? Light up her face? Since when do I notice shit like that?

He shook his head. He needed to move on. "Hey, sorry I'm late. Again."

Tiana moved over and patted the bench next to her. "It's okay. I just got here myself."

He looked at the few other groups of people. "I'm glad you picked a restaurant that's not busy," he said, taking his seat.

"Hall. Party of two," the hostess called out.

Tiana smiled and stood. "It's kind of a hidden gem. The food is good, but not many people know about it."

Ty got up, too. "Works for me. The sooner we get to our table, the sooner we eat."

Tiana looked over her shoulder at him as they followed the hostess to their table. "Hungry?"

"Yeah. I made some time to see your brother today. He decided he wanted to play basketball."

"How did that go?" she asked as they sat down at the table.

"Good. We were too busy playing to talk about much."

Thank God.

"So, what did you tell him about tonight and why you couldn't hang out?"

"I told him I had a date."

Tiana's eyes widened with panic. "You did?"

"Yes." He'd actually told Nate he had a date with the mother of his baby. However, he hadn't told Tiana that yet. Even though he'd left out the name of the mother, he didn't want to make her uncomfortable. "I figured he'd ask me less questions that way."

Despite their flirting the night before, he could tell that Tiana wasn't in the mood to continue tonight.

"What about you? How was your day?" he asked her.

She sighed. "It was good. Up until I was ready to leave to meet you."

"Oh?"

"My roommate and her boyfriend told me that I have two months to move out because he will be moving in."

Ty winced with sympathy.

"I was planning to move out anyway because of the baby. My roommate and I aren't close. I wouldn't expect her to put up with a newborn." She shrugged. "I just figured I'd have a little more time."

Ty wanted to tell her that she could move in with him. He had a three-bedroom house. It would be perfect. He could be with her and help her with things before the baby was born, and then they'd both be there after the baby came.

But he held his tongue. Something told him that Tiana wouldn't appreciate that offer. And he didn't blame her. They might have known each other for a few years, but they didn't *know* each other.

He didn't know her favorite color or her favorite food. And she didn't know his.

They might not even be compatible roommates. Ty thought back to his freshman roommate in college. The guy had been a total slob, and Ty had hated sharing a small space with him.

Yes, it was probably best not to bring up living together. At least for now. For both their sakes.

CHAPTER NINE

Monday morning, Tiana sat at her desk and stared at her computer screen. She should be working, but the weekend fog hadn't fully lifted.

Or it could be that she'd fried most of her brain cells the day before, looking for a place to live. She didn't remember apartment-hunting being that bad in the past.

She was also considering moving back in with her parents. But she couldn't ask about that until she told them about the baby. And she wasn't ready to do that yet.

The smart thing would be to move in first and then tell them she was pregnant. That way, they'd be around to help. It would make things easy for her, but it wouldn't be fair to them.

Tiana sighed.

"You okay over there?" her work neighbor, Alicia, asked.

Tiana spun her chair around. "No."

Alicia raised a dark eyebrow. It didn't match the purple on her head.

"My roommate's boyfriend is moving in."

Alicia curled her lip. "Have fun with that. Talk about being a third wheel."

Tiana slumped down in her seat. "Oh, no. They want me to move out."

Alicia's eyes widened. "Oh. That sucks."

"Yeah, but you're right. I wouldn't want to live there with the two of them. And it is Shannon's house. I totally understand." Tiana rested her head against the back. "It just could have come at a better time, is all."

"What's going on?"

Tiana studied Alicia. The two were work friends, but nothing more. They got along great but never did anything together outside of the office. And Tiana hadn't told anyone about the pregnancy besides Ty and her best friend, Jasmine, who lived in Denver. But she could tell Alicia about Ty. Alicia was about ten years older than Tiana and was kind of like a big sister. A work sister.

Tiana sat up. "This stays between us."

"Agreed." Alicia wiggled her eyebrows. "Now, tell me the dirt."

Tiana leaned closer to her friend. "At my brother's wedding, I slept with one of his groomsmen."

Alicia put her hand up. Even though Tiana rolled her eyes, she still high-fived it.

"Way to go, girl. Get your groove on."

"Shh," Tiana said with a laugh. "Someone's going to hear you."

It was Alicia's turn to roll her eyes. "So, how was it?" She nodded knowingly as a grin spread across her face. "He's got a big dick, doesn't he?"

Tiana's face heated.

"Oh, yeah, baby. Big dicks are all the rage."

"Alicia."

"What?"

"Little dicks aren't bad," Tiana said, feeling the need to defend the less popular–sized male anatomy.

"I know. I dated a guy who was on the smaller side, but he knew how to use it."

"See? I dated a guy who was big and therefore thought he didn't have to do anything."

"Okay, you made your point. Get back to your story. Was it good?"

"Yes."

"I *knew* it." Alicia adjusted in her seat. "Let me guess. You two have been hooking up this whole time, and now, you don't know what to think of your relationship."

Tiana shook her head. "No. We hadn't spoken since the wedding."

"Oh. Boo."

"But the weekend before last, we ran into each other again." If you counted Tiana going to Ty's house as running into him. "And we made plans for dinner last Saturday. The night before, we kind of sexted. Okay, not really. But there was definitely flirting going on."

"Ooh...so what happened on Saturday?"

"Nothing."

Alicia's shoulders slumped. "Oh."

"Yeah. With all his flirting by text, I thought that he was down for some more good times. Which I really could have used after finding out about my eviction. But all he did was give me a kiss on the temple and say good night."

"How did he seem during dinner?"

"Good. We talked. He listened. He didn't check his phone or his watch. And he was very sympathetic to my housing situation."

Alicia gave Tiana a look. "How long did you talk about getting kicked out?"

Tiana shrugged. "I don't know. For a while."

"And were you obviously upset when you told him?"

"Yeah."

"Hmm...maybe that's why he didn't flirt or hit on you."

"Yeah, maybe. But it sure would have been nice to have the distraction."

"Did you tell him that?"

"No." *Is Alicia crazy?* "I'm not going to tell him I want to have sex."

Alicia shrugged. "Maybe you should. It works for me."

Tiana had to admire her friend's boldness. "Huh."

"Text him now. Do some flirting. Let him know you're down for some sexy times."

"Really?"

"Yes, really. When I hit my second trimester, all my nausea ended, and I started getting horny. Who better than the father of the baby to scratch your itch?"

Tiana's eyes widened so far that she felt the air hit them. "I-I-I—"

Alicia laughed. "Save it. I see you every day, and I know a pregnant woman when I see one."

Tiana looked around. "Do you think everyone knows?" The thought of the whole office talking about her made her stomach ache.

Alicia reassuringly shook her head. "No. But I notice these things. I knew my sister was pregnant before she knew. It's like I have a sixth sense about it."

Tiana snorted in disbelief.

"Hey. Laugh all you want. I figured it out with you, didn't I?"

Tiana sighed. "You did."

"So, this guy is the father, right?"

"Yes."

"Then, you definitely need to hook up with him again. He's the reason you're pregnant. Now, it's his job to take care of you."

"Well, he did promise to take care of my cravings. Even in the middle of the night."

"There you go. Tell him you crave his dick. I'm sure he'd love to help."

Tiana laughed out loud and shook her head. It was a great line, but there was no way she'd ever use it on Ty.

Tiana went to grab her phone from the drawer she kept it in at the same moment her boss made an appearance. So, she quickly slammed the drawer closed, straightened in her chair, and put her fingers on her keyboard. Texting Ty would have to wait.

CHAPTER TEN

Ty had just pulled on some sweatpants when his doorbell rang. Not bothering to put on a shirt, he went to answer the door. Nate had asked Ty earlier if he was free tonight, and he'd surprised himself by saying yes right away.

But Ty had come to a couple of conclusions over the weekend. He wasn't going to feel any less guilty by not hanging out with one of his closest friends. And the guilt wasn't as strong as it had been when he first found out Tiana was pregnant.

Yes, Tiana was Nate's little sister, but it had really hit him that she was more than that. She was her own person. And she was an adult. Tiana didn't need her parents' permission, much less her brother's, to date and sleep with someone.

Ty knew Nate was going to be upset about the baby, but Ty was going to do everything he possibly could to be a good dad and a good co-parent.

Ready to spend some time with his friend, a little more

guilt-free, he swung open the door. But it wasn't Nate on the other side. It was Tiana.

"Hey."

"Heeeyyy," Tiana said, drawing out the word and letting it trail off as she stared at his chest.

He had to fight the urge to puff it out. He liked having her looking at him.

Ty checked his watch. They had a little bit of time before Nate was supposed to get there. "What's going on? Everything okay?"

"Uh..."

"Tiana."

She looked up at him with guilt in her eyes.

Ty couldn't help but chuckle. "Is everything okay with the baby?"

"Oh, yeah. I came to talk to you about something else."

Ty stepped back. "Come on in." Tiana entered, and he closed the door behind her. "So, what's going on?"

"Going on?"

Ty laughed. "I'm guessing you didn't come by just to say hi." He studied her face. "Are you sure everything is okay?"

"Do you like me?" she blurted out.

That seemed like an odd question. He thought they got along great, minus the fight they'd had the first time she came to his house.

"Of course I like you."

"No, I mean, do you *like* me?"

He rubbed the back of his neck. This was a tough question. "I honestly don't know how to answer that."

Tiana crossed her arms over her chest. "Try."

"Okay," he agreed hesitantly. He had a feeling this wasn't going to end up good for him.

She waved him on with a hand.

"I like you as a person. I had a lot of fun with you at your brother's wedding. I like you as a friend. I hope we continue to spend time together, especially since we're going to be co-parents. But I don't know how to answer if I like you in a romantic sense." He wasn't sure if he should keep going, but she'd said she wanted him to be honest the other night when they were texting. "Am I attracted to you? Hell yeah. Would I like to strip off all your clothes and bury myself inside you again? Fuck yes. But I don't know if that's the answer you're looking for."

Tiana grinned like the Cheshire cat and threw herself at him. She wrapped her arms around his neck and kissed him. Ty moaned into her mouth, and he slammed her against the wall.

God, she tastes good.

And that was when the doorbell rang.

Ty sprang away from Tiana in a panic. "That's your brother," he whispered.

"*What?*"

"Shh. He'll hear you."

There was a knock at the door.

Ty looked around. "Go to my room and hang out for a while. I'll try to get rid of him."

Tiana turned toward the bottom of the stairs, and he followed her.

"Which room is it?"

"End of the hall." He groaned. "Your car."

"I'm parked across the street." She bit her lip. "Hopefully, he won't notice it."

"Okay. Go, go, go. I'll get him to leave as soon as I can."

"Maybe I should sneak out the back. We can talk later."

Ty looked at the sliding glass doors. It did make more sense. He was about to agree when the door started to open. He gently pushed Tiana up the stairs and turned around as Nate entered the door Ty should have locked.

"Hey. I rang the bell and knocked."

Ty chuckled nervously. "Yeah. Sorry. I was upstairs, getting changed." He looked down at his chest. "I didn't even have time to put on a shirt."

Nate looked him up and down. "Are you sure? Because it looks like you were watching porn."

"Huh?"

Ty followed Nate's eyes to his crotch, and wouldn't you know it? He had a hard-on. Apparently, his fear of Nate catching them wasn't enough to get him to go soft.

"No, I wasn't watching porn. And stop staring at my dick."

Nate shrugged like he didn't believe him. "Whatever. I don't judge."

"I don't either. It's just that I wasn't doing that—"

Shut up, Ty. You are hiding his sister in your room.

"Never mind." He gestured toward the couch. "Do you want a beer?"

"Always." Nate plopped down on the couch and snatched up the TV remote.

Ty went to the kitchen to grab the two of them beers. He

also snagged a T-shirt he had hanging over the back of one of the kitchen chairs.

"I already ordered pizza," Nate called from the other room.

"Nice." Ty cursed to himself. *How am I going to get rid of him now?* He should have told Tiana to leave.

"Oh, and can you grab another beer? I invited Luke over. He could use a night off."

"Great." Ty closed the door and hung his head in defeat.

It was going to be a long night.

CHAPTER ELEVEN

To Ty, it felt like his friends had been at his house forever. He had managed to sneak some pizza up to his room for Tiana and check on her a couple times, but it hadn't been easy. His friends probably thought he had an UTI by the amount of times he had gone to the "bathroom."

Ty closed the door on Nate and Luke and sighed with relief. It was dark, so at least he didn't have to worry that Nate would notice his sister's car. As soon as the two of his friends drove away, he locked his door and ran up to his bedroom.

He pushed open his door. "I'm sorry it took so long. They wouldn't leave..."

Lying on top of his bed, Tiana was fast asleep. He glanced at the bedside clock and saw that it was after ten.

He remembered when his sister had been pregnant. She had been tired all the time, so Ty knew Tiana needed her rest. Tomorrow was a workday, and there would be no sleeping in.

He very gently pulled down the covers from under her and covered her up before turning off the light on his nightstand. He used the light from the TV to find his bathroom and some clothes for the next morning. That way, he could use the bathroom in the hall and sleep on the couch.

He had two extra bedrooms, but he used one as his office and the other for miscellaneous storage. He might have to take his mom's advice and finally get an extra bed.

He pulled off his T-shirt and threw it into the laundry basket in the corner. He walked to his dresser, picked out a clean tee, and turned off the television before tiptoeing to the door. He was just about to slip into the hall when he heard Tiana move around on the bed.

"Ty?" Her voice was low and full of sleep.

He stepped back into the room. "Yeah?" he whispered.

"What time is it?"

"It's late. After ten. I'm going to sleep in the living room. What time do you need to be up for work? I'll set my alarm."

Tiana sat up. "I have to be at work at eight. I should probably get up at six."

"Six it is." He smiled. "Have a good night." He pivoted again.

"Ty?"

"Yeah?"

"Will you lie with me?"

"Uh..." He didn't bother to turn back to her yet. "I'm not sure if that's a good idea."

"Please. I'm alone in a strange room."

He looked back at her.

"Just until I fall asleep. You can escape after that."

Ty laughed and walked toward the bed. "Hey. That's not nice. I don't want to escape."

"Then, get your butt in bed."

He flipped the other side of the covers down when he remembered what he was wearing. "Do you want me to put a shirt on?"

"Not on your life."

Ty chuckled as he slipped into bed beside her. He wrapped an arm around Tiana and drew her close.

Tiana woke from a deep and restful sleep for the second time that night. She lay on her side with a strong arm around her waist and the warmth of a big male body behind her.

She remembered that body.

The night of her brother's wedding, she and Ty had fallen asleep after a couple rounds of sex. When she'd woken in the middle of the night, she'd turned to him, and he'd pulled her into his open arms.

She wondered which time that night she'd gotten pregnant. They'd used condoms every time without problems, so she could only guess.

She peeked up at the clock to see that it was only after one in the morning. She had a few hours left before she needed to be up for the day.

She gently rolled over and faced Ty. Her eyes were adjusted to the dark, and she was close, so she could see the features on his face. There was something handsome about a man sleeping.

She softly touched his collarbone. "Ty?" she whispered.

He didn't move.

She applied a little more pressure and trailed her fingers down to his chest. "Ty," she said again, a little louder.

He put his hand on top of hers. "Everything okay?" he asked without opening his eyes.

No. She was horny. But she knew he wasn't asking about that. "Everything is okay with the baby. You'll have to stop asking me that, or everything's not going to be okay with you."

An eye popped open. Just one. "Meaning?"

"Meaning, I might snap from being asked the same thing over and over."

Ty opened both eyes and smiled. "Noted." His lids shut again, and his hand relaxed around hers.

She scooted nearer to him and put her face so close to his that their noses almost touched. "I do have a minor problem though."

The one eye opened again, and the corner of his mouth lifted. "Oh, yeah? And what's that?"

Tiana pulled her hand out from under his and trailed it down his torso until she hit the seam of his pants. "I need something."

"Hmm...I'm guessing it's not ice cream or pickles."

"It's not food." She grinned. "But I can put it in my mouth."

The second eye flew open. "Fuck." He groaned and rolled onto his back. "Why did you have to say that?" Ty sounded like he was in pain. "Now, I'm picturing your mouth wrapped around my dick."

Tiana laughed. "That's kind of the point. But full confession?"

He turned his head and looked at her. "Yes?"

"I'd rather have you take off all my clothes and bury yourself inside me."

Ty ran a thumb down her cheek. "No wonder I found it so hard to resist you."

"What do you mean?"

"I was beating myself up a little for sleeping with you and getting you pregnant. But then I realized something."

"Oh? What was that?"

He turned back to her. "That you're an adult woman who can decide for herself what she wants," he said as he tugged her toward him and took her mouth.

"Mmm..." she moaned against his lips before slipping her tongue into his mouth.

Ty ran his hands down her back and cupped her ass. He yanked her lower half to him and pushed his hard length against the seam of her pussy.

She could already feel herself getting wet and her clit swelling. Hormones and pregnancy were serious stuff.

Ty rubbed her swollen nub over his dick, and soon, she had to pull her mouth away from his to catch her breath.

"Oh God," she said, clutching his shoulders. "I think...I think...oh shit...I'm going to *cooooooome...*" she yelled out the last word as her orgasm took over her body.

Ty rolled her onto her back, so he could grind against her harder, which only prolonged her climax.

When her body stopped shaking and she came back to herself, she put her hands on his shoulders.

Ty rested his body on his elbows and smiled down at her. "You weren't expecting that, were you?"

She shook her head and laughed breathlessly. "Not at all."

"Some of the best orgasms hit you by surprise."

CHAPTER TWELVE

The rest of the week dragged on for what felt like forever. She was sick of work, she was sick of looking for a place to rent, and she really wanted to see Ty again.

After he'd given her an orgasm Monday night, he'd taken her into his arms and told her to sleep.

Sleep? She hadn't wanted to go to sleep. She'd wanted to have sex.

But apparently, her body had assumed it knew better than her mind because that was her last thought before Ty woke her up in the morning.

She'd rushed out of his house so quickly to make it to work on time that she'd barely said good-bye.

She needed to keep her mind off of him and her vajayjay.

She turned in her chair to face Alicia. "When did you start your baby registry?"

Tiana was hoping to go to Target that weekend and look at baby things. All her friends were going out and doing stuff, and since she couldn't, she thought making the registry would be fun. She also needed a break from apartment-shopping.

Her coworker pushed a few buttons on her keyboard and spun to face her. "I honestly can't remember. That was seven years ago."

"Do you think it would be too early to make one? I'm not even halfway through my pregnancy yet."

Alicia thought about it and then shook her head. "No. I don't think I would tell anyone about it yet in case something happens, but I see no harm in making one." She grinned. "It's fun. It's like shopping, but you don't have to spend any money." She frowned. "But what about clothes? Are you going gender neutral, or are you waiting until you find out what you're having and going back to pick out some boy or girl stuff?"

Tiana shrugged. "Maybe I'll get all three. In case you haven't heard, gender is fluid."

Alicia raised her eyebrows.

Tiana waved her away. "Besides, all that *pink is for girls and blue is for boys* is an American thing. I even read an article that said gender-specific clothes didn't happen until the mid-nineteenth century. And at one time, blue was recommended for girls and pink for boys. The whole thing is stupid. I'm going to buy stuff that I think is cute."

Alicia nodded once and said, "Good idea. It is a little stupid to think boys and girls can't wear each other's clothes. What's the worst that could happen? It's not like it's going to kill anybody."

"Exactly."

Alicia turned to her computer and typed for a minute or so. "Have you thought about asking Ty to go with you?"

Tiana wrinkled her nose. "Not really. He's a guy. Guys don't like shopping."

Alicia burst out laughing.

"What's so funny?"

"You just told me that gender-specific stuff is stupid. And now, you're assuming something about Ty just because he's a guy."

Tiana sighed. "You're right."

"Besides, even if Ty doesn't like shopping, he might want to do it because it's something for the baby."

"Hmm..."

Tiana turned back to her desk and pulled out her phone.

> Tiana: I was thinking of doing the baby registry this weekend.

> Ty: Sounds like fun.

> Tiana: Would you like to go with me?

> Ty: Sure. But aren't you going to look at more places this weekend?

> Tiana: *sigh* I only have one that I'm looking at Saturday morning, and I'm not hopeful.

> Ty: Oh.

> Tiana: It's far from work. It's far from my parents. And it's far from you. Even if I like it, I don't want to do that much driving.

> Ty: I don't blame you.

> Ty: Maybe you should ask someone if you can rent a room in their house.

She immediately thought of her brother. But he and Piper were about to have their own baby. She didn't want to be in their way, and she didn't know how they'd feel about her bringing a baby with her.

> Tiana: I think I'll pass for now. It's a good idea. I just don't think that's something I want to do at the moment.

Ty stared down at his phone. He guessed she'd told him. It was a good thing he hadn't come out and asked her. He'd have felt like a fool.

Maybe, this weekend, they needed to start talking about custody. He knew they had a while to go, but he'd like to plant the idea in her brain, so she could think about it. Plus, he needed her to know that he wanted to spend as much time with the baby as possible. He didn't want her to worry that he would think the child was a burden. Not that she did think that, but it was a good idea to make sure.

> Ty: What time do you want to meet on Saturday?

He'd already been turned down once today, and he wasn't sure if he wanted to be turned down again, so he went for it.

Ty: I can go with you to look at the apartment, and then we can go do the registry after that. Maybe do lunch, too.

Tiana: That sounds perfect. It's always nice to have a second set of eyes.

Ty: How about I pick you up in the morning?

Tiana: Great. Looking forward to it.

Now, that was a much better reaction.

CHAPTER THIRTEEN

Ty turned to the landlord. "Can you give us a minute?"

He could tell that Tiana was upset and frustrated, but she was too polite to say anything in front of the stranger.

The older gentleman nodded. "Take your time. I'll be right outside."

After the door closed behind him, Ty turned to Tiana. "You hate it, don't you?" But it was more than that. Most people would say, *No, thank you,* and move on to the next place.

She fell back against the wall and sank down to the worn and old carpet. She put her head in her hands. "I didn't realize how much I had been counting on this place. I know I told you yesterday that I wasn't expecting anything great, but apparently, my subconscious was."

Ty sat down next to her and put his arm around her. She smelled delicious, and he liked having her close to him.

When she didn't hesitate to lay her head on his shoulder, he couldn't help but smile. "So, tell me what's wrong."

"The place is ancient and run-down. And it's not even as close to work as I thought it might be." She plucked at the brown carpet. "At least it's clean."

"I'll give the place that. And the landlord seems nice."

"He does. It's just...I thought I could get more for my money. It looks like I'm going to have to move farther out, or I'm going to have to really pinch my pennies."

Ty had a silent war going on in his head. He wanted to ask her to move in with him. But he wasn't sure if now was the time. He didn't want her to think he was asking because he felt sorry for her, and he didn't want her to say yes because she was upset.

Tiana lifted her head and sighed. "We might as well take the man's card and get out of here. I'm ready for some good stuff. Shopping and food. I can worry about this whole living situation later."

Tiana used the gun to scan the next item she wanted for her registry and laughed. "This is fun." She turned to look at Ty. "What's become of me? I'm turning into a loser," she joked.

Ty laughed. "I think it's called getting older."

"Whatever you say." She looked down to the paper he was holding. "What else is on the baby registry suggestion list?"

Ty listed a few choices. "Which one should we do?"

"Let's look at cribs and bedding."

"Sounds good."

They went to the aisle with the blankets, sheets, and accessories that she'd had no idea she needed for a baby.

"Do I need one of these things, so the baby doesn't fall out of the crib?"

"Not right away. But once the baby starts moving, it's a good idea. It helps keep their legs, arms, and the occasional head from getting stuck between the rails."

Tiana spun around to look at Ty. "How do you know this?"

"I have two nieces."

"I didn't know that. You didn't say anything."

Ty shrugged. "Sorry. I only see them a few times a year. My brother-in-law's job transferred him to Virginia a couple of years ago, so unfortunately, I don't see them as much as I'd like to."

"That sucks."

He shrugged again. "It does. But maybe, someday, they'll get to move back to Minnesota."

Tiana scanned Ty up and down. He looked so manly next to all the baby stuff, and she felt a tingle shiver through her body. Hearing him talk so confidently about his knowledge of babies made him even sexier.

She moved down the aisle. "What are their names?"

"Who?"

She laughed. "Your nieces."

"Oh. Monica and Brandy."

"That's nice."

Ty stopped walking. "It was a joke."

Tiana frowned. "I don't get it."

"Way to make me feel old."

"I'm sorry?" she said questioningly because she had no idea how she'd insulted him.

"Brandy and Monica were both singers. They did a song together called 'The Boy Is Mine.' I was a freshman in high school, I think." Ty pulled out his phone and punched the song into the search bar. "It came out in 1998."

Now, Tiana really did feel bad. "I was a little kid. That's why I don't remember."

He slapped his hand on his forehead. "Your brother is going to kill me. I'm so much older than you."

Tiana patted him on the chest. "Nah. He wouldn't kill his niece or nephew's father. He might hurt you though."

Ty dropped his hand. "Thanks. That makes me feel so much better," he said sarcastically.

Tiana laughed. "So, what are your nieces' real names?"

"Layla and Evie."

"Cute. I'd better take those names off my list."

His brow furrowed. "Were they on your list?"

"Nah. I'm waiting to see if the baby is a boy or a girl."

Ty bit his lip. "Do I get any say on this list?"

He looked so nervous and cute as he asked the question; Tiana didn't have the heart to tease him like she wanted to.

"Yes."

He grinned.

She held her finger up. "But I get final say. If I don't like a name, we're not compromising."

"Does that mean Tyler Morgan Jr. is an option?"

Tiana laughed and then looked at him with a straight face. "Hell no."

Ty frowned. "Why not?"

"Too confusing."

"Why? I can be Ty, and our son can be Tyler."

Tiana shook her head. "No way. I had a coworker who had the same name as his dad with a different middle name. They were always getting each other's mail, and worse, their credit scores were messed up because my coworker's dad was a gambler. It's really hard to fix that stuff." She shook her head again. "In this day and age, with everything on the computer, I'm not risking it. Our son—if we have a son—is going to have his own name."

Ty stared at her and burst out laughing.

She put her hands on her hips. "What's so funny?"

"I'm sorry. You were just so serious about that."

"I'm an accountant. Your credit score and finances *are* serious." She grabbed the handle of the cart and kept walking.

"Hold up. I'm sorry. You're right."

Tiana stopped and scowled at him over her shoulder for laughing at her. "Does this mean that you have a terrible credit score?"

Ty's smile was gone in a flash and replaced with a scowl. "Of course not."

"Ha. See, it's important to you, too." Tiana turned forward again and smiled to herself. It was good to know the father of her baby was responsible with money.

Tiana stopped at some bedding she liked. It had elephants on it, and the colors were gray, pink, and blue. It would work for a boy or a girl. "I like this one. What do you think?"

Ty shrugged. "It's cute."

"Which one would you pick?" she asked, spreading her arm out in front of herself at all the choices on the shelf.

"I don't know. This one is fine," he said, pointing to the one she picked.

"Fine?"

He laughed. "Ti, I'm a guy. I don't care what it looks like as long as it serves its purpose."

"Then, it's a good thing you're not picking it out."

Everything was going to match in her child's nursery. It was going to be pretty and homey and the perfect place for her child to sleep. But another thought occurred to her, and she gasped.

Ty's eyes widened. "What?"

"I just realized we need to double up on stuff on the registry, so we can have one of everything at each of our places. Otherwise, we're going to be lugging a lot of stuff around." She made a disappointed sound. "Ugh. We've already looked at so many things. I don't want to go back."

Ty rubbed his chin but didn't say anything.

"What?" she asked. "I can tell you're thinking something."

"You're going to think I'm crazy."

"Okay," she said, as if that should matter. "And?"

"We agreed we're going to raise this child together, correct?"

"Yeah."

"I was thinking..."

"What?" she asked when he didn't continue.

"I worry it's too soon to bring this up."

She raised her brow. "Too late. You have to say it now."

He took a deep breath. "I was thinking you need a place to live. I have three bedrooms—four if you count the one in the basement. So, why don't you move in with me?"

He wants to live together? As a couple?

They didn't know each other that well despite the baby growing inside her.

"You can have the spare room. I'll move my office downstairs, so the baby can have the third bedroom."

Oh. He meant live together as roommates. She wasn't sure if she was disappointed or relieved. But it definitely did make more sense.

"What do you say?" he asked.

It was an answer to all her problems. While she had the fleeting thought, *If it's too good to be true, it probably is*, she'd been searching for a place to live with zero success. She might be making a mistake, but she figured, *What the hell?*

She met Ty's eyes. "Let's do it."

CHAPTER FOURTEEN

Tiana dropped her last box on her new bedroom floor and sighed with relief. "And moving day is complete." She still had to make her bed and put her bathroom stuff away before she went to sleep that night, but the rest could wait until after she was rested.

"Yay," Jasmine said through Tiana's Bluetooth headset. "I'm sorry I couldn't be there to help."

"Girl, I told you, it's fine. I had basically one room—*one room*—to move. Now, if it had been a whole house, I'd have expected your ass to be here, new job or no new job."

Jasmine laughed. "Hey, you know I want to be there."

"I know. But not to help me move. You want to scope out Ty."

"And?"

It was Tiana's turn to laugh.

"How are things going with Mr. Older Man anyway?"

"He went to drop off the U-Haul and run some errands. As for how things are going..." Tiana shrugged even though her friend couldn't see her. "Good. He did offer me a place to live, didn't he?"

Jasmine clicked her tongue. "You know that's not what I meant."

Tiana spun around and dropped her butt to her bed. "No. There's been some flirting, but that's it." She bit her lip. "God, I hope he's not sleeping with a bunch of women, and that's why he hasn't made a move on me."

"Hey, you'll find out soon enough."

"*Jasmine.*"

"What? It's true. You're living together now. Either you'll see him bring home girls or not come home at all."

"Or maybe neither of those things will happen."

"Maybe." Jasmine didn't sound convinced.

"I'm sorry. I have to go now. My best friend is being a—"

"*Hey.*"

Tiana grinned. "You don't know what I was going to say."

"I can imagine."

"Do you want me to tell you?" Tiana teased.

"No. When was the bedroom incident?"

"Incident? You make it sound like an accident."

"When was it?"

"It'll be two weeks on Monday."

"And how much time have you spent together?"

"I don't know." Tiana shrugged. "We hung out last weekend."

"When you looked at that crappy apartment and went shopping for baby stuff?"

"Technically, it was for the baby registry, but yes."

"How did that day end? Remind me."

Tiana closed her eyes and remembered Ty dropping her off at her now-old house. "He pulled up to the driveway and said good-bye."

She had thought he would at least lean in for a kiss, but that hadn't happened.

"Did he shut off the engine?" Jasmine asked.

"No." She opened her eyes. "But he did put the car in park."

"Did you invite him in?"

"No."

"Woman, how is he supposed to know that you want him to come in and have sex with you if you don't invite him in?"

"Shut up, Jasmine. Nobody asked you."

"You literally brought the subject up first."

Tiana's earpiece beeped. She jumped off the bed and looked around her room, having forgotten where she'd laid her phone. The light from the screen shone through the papers she had set on top of it. Pushing them aside, she saw that it was her brother.

She lifted a shoulder. She'd call him back.

"I had another call," Tiana said. "What were we talking about?"

"You need to let the man know you're interested."

"Why doesn't he let me know he's interested in me?"

"Does he have a penis?"

"Yes."

"He's interested in you."

Tiana shook her head. "Jasmine, not every guy wants to have sex with every girl."

"Okay then, did he invite you to live with him?"

"Yes."

"He's interested."

"I don't know."

"Who is returning the U-Haul you rented to move your stuff?"

"Ty."

"He's interested."

They were good points, but Tiana wasn't sure even though she was hopeful.

A beep sounded in her ear once more. It was Nate again.

"Hey, I have to go."

"Trying to get rid of me because I speak the truth?"

Tiana laughed. "No. My brother has called twice now. It's probably important."

"It's probably the baby."

"Eek," she shrieked with excitement. "I've gotta go."

She switched calls, hanging up before Jasmine could even say good-bye.

"Hello?"

"Are you ready to come and meet your nephew? He came a little early," Nate said.

"Yes. You know I've been dying to."

Nate laughed. "When can you get here?"

"I need to shower. I just got done moving."

After the words left her mouth, she realized that she hadn't told her family she'd found a different place to live or that the place was Ty's.

It was a good thing her brother hadn't even noticed. "Okay. Don't rush. We'll still be here when you get to the hospital."

CHAPTER FIFTEEN

Tiana stared down at the face of her brand-new nephew and fell in love. If she was this head over heels for her brother's kid, she couldn't imagine how she was going to feel when she met her own.

Her knees felt weak, so she took herself and the baby to the nearest chair.

"You okay?" Nate asked. "You're not going to drop the baby, are you?"

She shot her brother a look. "No. I was only thinking of how much I love him already, and I just met him."

Piper sniffled.

Nate spun around to his wife. "What's wrong?"

"Nothing," she said in a shaky voice. "It's just so sweet." Piper looked at Tiana. "Hormones," she explained.

Yikes. She wasn't looking forward to that. She looked back down into her nephew's sweet face. It would all be worth it though.

"Does this little guy have a name yet?" Tiana asked.

Nate cleared his throat, and Tiana looked up in time to see him make eye contact with Piper. "I think so."

She smiled at her husband. "He does."

Nate's face went from anticipation to relief.

Tiana chuckled. "Don't leave me hanging. What is it?"

The two exchanged looks again.

"We kind of want to wait for everyone to get here," Nate said.

"You're killin' me." They'd already made her wait the whole pregnancy. "Who's everyone?"

"Dad and Tricia at least."

Two people? She could wait. "As your child's only aunt, I think I have a right to know now," she teased.

Nate rolled his eyes. "Fine."

Tiana held up her hand. "I'm joking. You can wait for everyone to get here." She looked down at her nephew. "Until they get here, I'll just call you Baby Hall."

Her stomach did a somersault. Would her baby be a Hall, too? Or a Morgan? It was still early, but she and Ty hadn't discussed last names at all. When was the appropriate time to bring *that* subject up?

There were footsteps and voices getting closer to Piper's room, saving Tiana from having to worry about what last name she was going to give her unborn child. A few seconds later, her parents walked through the door.

"Congratulations," their dad said as soon as he saw Nate and Piper.

"Thanks, Dad."

Her mom handed Piper a gift bag. "Sorry we didn't get

here right away. I made Jerome stop at the store, so I could get the baby a gift."

"You didn't have to do that," Piper said.

"Hush now. This is my first grandchild. I'm giving him a gift." Her mother did a full turn. "Now, where is the little guy?"

She was so busy looking for the baby that she didn't see Nate's face at the mention of a grandchild, but Tiana noticed. She knew Nate and her mother had had troubles before she was born, and it warmed her heart to know that her mom accepted the baby as she would Tiana's baby when it came.

Her mom noticed Tiana sitting in the corner and rushed over with her arms out. "It's my turn."

Tiana gently moved the baby from her arms to her mother's.

"Honey?" her mom said with concern.

Tiana looked up. "Yeah?"

"Why are you crying?"

She wiped her cheek. She hadn't even realized. "I'm so happy, I guess," she said with a smile. She almost added, *Hormones*, to copy Piper, but she didn't want to steal her nephew's thunder.

Plus, her brother was beaming. Today was not the day to ruin a friendship.

Piper handed Tiana a box of tissues with that look of speculation she'd been getting on her face a lot recently. "You sure you're okay?"

Tiana laughed as she snatched a couple of tissues. "Yes. A little emotional, I suppose. This is my first encounter as an aunt."

Piper pursed her lips. "Mmhmm," was all she said.

Tiana was saved again as Luke and Ty walked into the room. Upon seeing the father of her baby, she couldn't help but feel a little calmer.

The two men clapped hands with her brother and did a half-hug, half-back slap move as Tiana got up from her seat.

"You sit, Mom," she said. It was only right that she let her mother sit since she was the one who had the baby, but she also wanted to be closer to Ty.

"Where's Elise?" Piper asked.

"With Lili. We couldn't find someone to watch her, and Elise didn't know if she should bring the baby to the hospital."

"I think it would have been fine," Nate said. "After all, she should meet her future husband."

Luke scowled. "She will never be getting married. No man is ever touching her."

"Even if it's my son?" Nate pretended to be offended, but he was trying not to smile.

"Especially your son. I grew up with you, man. You can't trust a Hall man."

Tiana exchanged looks with Ty. She assumed he was thinking the same thing she was. That Hall men weren't the only ones who couldn't be trusted.

Tiana grinned at him and had to bite her lip before everyone else saw.

Ty smiled as he lowered his head and shook it.

"Hey!" Tiana's father's deep voice made her jump, but then she realized he was responding to what Luke had just said.

Luke cleared his throat. "Except for you, sir."

Jerome laughed. "I'm messing with you, Luke." He put his hand up to his mouth as if he were telling a secret to the younger man, but he didn't bother to lower his voice when he said, "If my grandson is anything like my son, I don't blame you if you keep him away from your daughter."

"Thanks, Dad," Nate said, his voice dripping with sarcasm.

Jerome laughed again. "That's what dads are for."

"I'll have you know, our little Wyatt would never do anything to hurt Lili."

Tiana's ears perked up at this. "Wyatt?"

"Oops." Nate smiled at his wife.

Piper threw up her hands and rolled her eyes. "Might as well tell them."

Nate took the baby from Tiana's mom and moved to Piper's side. He reached down and grasped her hand. "Everyone, I'd like you to meet Wyatt Jordan."

The room went silent as everyone processed that the baby's middle name was after Piper's late husband and Nate's late friend.

Tiana decided to break the silence. "That's the sweetest thing I've ever heard," she said as she started to cry again.

Ty put his arm around her while everyone was looking at Nate and Piper, and she leaned into him, giving herself one comforting moment before they separated. She stepped away and looked out of the corner of her eye at him as she sat down next to her mom.

This secret-business stuff sucked.

CHAPTER SIXTEEN

Ty picked up Nate's baby and was in awe. He couldn't believe he was going to have one of his own soon.

His heart skipped a beat at the thought. He was excited and overwhelmed at the same time.

Ty snuck a look at the person growing his baby and almost dropped little Wyatt.

He was shocked the hospital room hadn't caught on fire with the amount of heat coming out of her eyes. She looked like she wanted to fuck him right then and there. Her family in the room be damned.

Since Wyatt was snuggled safely in his left arm, Ty reached for his phone in his back pocket and sent off a text.

> Ty: If you don't stop looking at me with fuck-me eyes, everyone in this room is going to know we have something going on.

Tiana's phone pinged, and she picked it up out of her purse. Her eyes widened a moment later.

> Tiana: I can't help it. It is soooo sexy, watching you hold that baby.

> Ty: It must be a biological thing.

> Tiana: Whatever it is, it is turning me on. I'm going to need to find a private room soon, so I can…relieve some pressure.

> Ty: You'd better not.

Tiana's eyebrows flew up.

> Ty: I mean, I'd rather you wait for me.

"What do you think?" Nate walked over and asked.

Ty quickly turned off his screen and shoved his phone back in his pocket as Nate slapped him on the back.

"You ready for one of those yourself someday?"

From the other side of the room, a coughing fit broke out. Tiana had a water bottle in her hand and was pounding her chest.

"Are you okay?" Tricia asked her.

Tiana nodded, and Ty looked at Nate. "You know I am."

Nate didn't know the whole story about his past, but he knew enough.

"Hey, whatever happened with that girl who thought she might be pregnant?" Nate said in a low voice.

Ty shook his head. He'd regretted ever bringing it up in the first place, and now was not the time to talk about it.

Nate slapped him again, gentler this time. "It'll happen someday, man. I'm sure of it."

Nate had misunderstood his head shake, and Ty felt bad, but he was going to leave it at that. The less questions asked by Nate, the better.

Ty tried his best not to look at Tiana again, but it was really hard. Nate had no idea how soon that *someday* was.

Little Wyatt started to fuss, clearing Ty's thoughts. "Hey, bud. It's okay."

"I think he's hungry," Piper said.

Ty looked down at the baby. "Me, too, buddy. I haven't had anything to eat since I helped Tiana move in this morning."

The room went silent, and Ty raised his head. Tiana's eyes were as wide as saucers, and he realized he'd messed up.

She had told him that she wanted to be the one to tell her brother she was moving into his house, so he hadn't brought it up all week at work, but he'd been surprised Nate hadn't either. Now, he knew why. She hadn't told him.

Ty looked at Jerome and Tricia. They looked as confused as Nate, who slowly turned around to his sister, head cocked to the side.

"What does Ty mean?"

Tiana still looked panicked, so Ty answered for her, "Your sister told me that she needed a place to live. I had an extra bedroom, so I offered it to her." He shrugged as if it weren't a big deal.

Nate narrowed his eyes. "I don't know if I want my sister living with you."

"Yes, honey," Tricia said, "are you sure about having a man as a roommate?"

Tiana finally seemed to snap out of it. "You guys, it's fine. Nate and Ty are friends. You trust Ty, right, Nate?"

"I don't know," Nate said, scrutinizing Ty.

Ty had to keep his breathing even and remind himself that no one knew he'd had sex with Tiana.

"Nate," Tiana said.

Nate rolled his eyes. "Okay, okay. Of course I trust Ty. I wouldn't have had him in my wedding otherwise."

"See, Mom? It's fine. And he'll probably be a better roommate than Shannon."

"I certainly won't kick you out because my boyfriend is moving in," Ty joked.

"You'll just make her want to move out after you bring a bunch of women home," Nate joked back.

Ty scowled at his friend. He didn't want Tiana getting the wrong idea. "I'm not a man-whore, like you," he tried to say in the same tone as before, but it was hard since he was getting mad now.

"Dude"—Nate pointed to his dad and stepmom—"parents."

Ty smiled sheepishly at the older couple. "Sorry."

Jerome burst out laughing. It was a good thing the man had a sense of humor.

Tiana rolled her eyes. "You all act like I don't know what sex is. I'm twenty-four years old. If Ty brings a woman home, I think I can handle it."

She said that a little too nonchalantly for Ty's taste.

"And my husband is no longer a manwhore," Piper added.

Nate grinned. "Just for you, I am."

Tiana shoved a finger in her open mouth like she was going to throw up, and everyone laughed, except Wyatt. He let out a loud yell to let the group know he did not like being forgotten.

Nate clapped his hands. "All right, people, clear the room. The baby is hungry, and no one gets to see my lady's boobs but me."

Piper snorted as Tiana said, "Gross."

"Just get out," Nate said to Tiana. "Or I'll really show you what gross is."

"Children," Jerome interrupted, "stop fighting."

Tiana rose from her chair and held up her hands. "I'm innocent in all this." She stuck her tongue out at Nate and ran out of the room.

Ty handed Piper the baby and walked out with the rest of them as his phone buzzed again.

> Tiana: That was close.

"Should we wait?" Tricia asked Jerome as they all gathered in the hall. "We didn't really say good-bye."

> Ty: Sorry. I didn't realize you hadn't said anything.

> Tiana: It's okay. Everyone knows now, so it's kind of a relief. One less secret to keep.

Ty: Just so you know, I won't be bringing any women home.

He waited for a reply, but when he didn't get one, he looked up at Tiana.

She smiled at him knowingly. The heat was back in her eyes.

"Well, I think I'm going to head out," Ty said. "I'll text Nate good-bye. I still have some things I have to take care of today."

Luke held his hand out, and Ty shook it. Luke turned to Tiana's parents, so Ty took the opportunity to give Tiana's butt a small smack on the way to the elevator.

"What was that for?" she whispered as he passed.

Ty took a step toward her and put his mouth near her ear. "That's for teasing me...again." He grinned. "Next time, you might not be so lucky." He nipped at her lobe and walked away.

He heard Tiana clear her throat behind him. "I'm going to head out, too."

"Oh?" Jerome asked. "Did you two ride together?"

"Nope," Tiana answered. "But I have things to do, too."

Ty hoped that he was on her to-do list.

CHAPTER SEVENTEEN

As Tiana drove back to Ty's house—her *home*; she needed to start thinking of it as home—she thought about what he'd said to her before they left the hospital.

"That's for teasing me...again."

She could not figure out what he'd meant by that. She didn't remember teasing him. If anything, he'd been the one teasing her, looking all sexy while he'd held her new nephew.

She'd tried to catch up to him in the elevator, but he was gone when she got there. She hadn't seen him as she walked to her car, so she had been left wondering.

It was a conundrum for sure. And she probably would have obsessed about it the whole drive, except she drove past a doughnut shop and had a sudden craving.

She hadn't even known she wanted a doughnut, and she felt like she might go crazy if she didn't put one in her mouth *right now*.

She rounded the next corner, so she could turn around

and go back to the store to satisfy her sudden hunger. *This has to be a pregnancy craving.* She might as well buy more than one.

♡

Tiana looked in her rearview mirror as she used a napkin to wipe the last of the chocolate icing off her face. Ty didn't need to know that she'd practically inhaled that thing, nearly swallowing it whole.

She rubbed her belly. "I hope you're happy, baby. Because I cannot eat another bite of sugar at the moment."

There was no response, of course, but she was excited for the day when she might get a kick or a punch in return.

She smiled to herself as she walked up to the door, so lost in her baby thoughts that she was unprepared to be pulled inside and pushed against the wall.

Ty's lips came down on hers, and he soul-kissed her, sucking all thoughts from her brain, except for the one about how good he tasted.

Tiana slipped her hands under his shirt, feeling the smooth skin of his ripped abs and then the muscular pecs above his six-pack. She thumbed his nipples, and he groaned into her mouth.

She broke their kiss as she smiled widely at her victory in getting a reaction out of him. As Ty smiled back, he wrapped his hands behind her legs and picked her up.

Tiana shrieked. "What are you doing?"

"Taking you upstairs, where I can have my way with you."

She nuzzled his neck and kissed him there. "Promise?"

"Promise."

"You'd better keep your word."

They reached the top of the stairs as he chuckled. "You make it sound like this is all a hardship for me. Baby, there is nothing I want more than to be inside you."

Ty walked through his bedroom door and gently laid her on his bed before standing and pulling off his shirt.

"I think you should go shirtless all the time."

He is beautiful.

Ty lifted an eyebrow. "I'll take your word for it."

"Ooh...sexy and modest."

"And hungry. Take your pants off."

Tiana grinned as she kicked her pants off, yanked her shirt over her head, and got rid of her bra and underwear. She was starting to get a little belly from the baby, but she happened to find it cute and wasn't at all embarrassed to be seen naked with it.

She hoped Ty would keep his head in the game. If he started thinking about the baby when they were supposed to be having sex, she was going to be one cranky woman. The last time they'd messed around, they hadn't had sex. She wasn't going to let that happen again. She hadn't had sex in months...and she was due.

Ty pushed down his pants, and his beautiful, dark dick sprang free of his boxers.

Tiana licked her lips.

She was so focused on that part of his anatomy, she barely noticed Ty kicking his jeans to the side or that he was completely naked until he landed on top of her lower half.

She leaned forward to pull him up to her, but before she could reach him, he pushed one of her legs toward her shoulder and licked the seam of her vagina.

She fell back against the bed, panting. "What was that for?"

"I told you, I was hungry."

"I thought you meant for sex." She lifted her head to meet Ty's eyes.

He snickered. "Yeah, I'm hungry for that, too. But first, I'm going to feast on your pussy."

"That's not fair—"

He leaned down and sucked her clit into his mouth. After about thirty seconds or twelve years—she really couldn't tell with all the sensations coursing through her body—he lifted his head.

"What were you saying?"

She mumbled something. She wasn't even sure what she'd said.

Ty chuckled. "That's what I thought." And he lowered his head again and went back to work.

CHAPTER EIGHTEEN

After Ty felt like Tiana was good and satisfied, he crawled up her body. He brushed back some hair that had stuck to her face from the sweat that gathered. "You okay?"

She nodded and nudged his hand away. "I'm kind of gross now."

His smile fell, and he looked her in the eyes. "Never. It just means I did my job right."

She smiled and opened her legs, so he fell between them, his dick sliding over her very wet pussy. "I'd say you did half your job right," she said with a teasing grin.

He raised his brow. "Half a job? Should I be insulted?"

She wrapped her arms around his neck. "Not even close. But you did promise to fuck me, so that means your job isn't done." She lifted her pelvis and rubbed her wetness over him.

He hissed and cursed.

"Was that English?" Tiana joked.

Ty laughed.

She grinned up at him and brushed herself against him again.

"Wait. Condom."

Tiana laughed and put her mouth next to his ear. "Want to hear a secret?"

"Yes."

She kissed down his neck and then back up to his ear once more. "I'm already pregnant. You don't need to use a condom."

Her secret was nothing new, but hearing her say it out loud made his dick even harder than it already had been. He groaned and moved his head, so he could kiss her.

After she was successfully breathless, he lifted his head. "I love the thought of being inside you bare, but I should get tested first." He knew it was the right thing to do, but his dick wasn't liking it.

Without warning, Tiana pushed him off her and onto his back. And before he knew which way was up, she straddled his hips and sank down onto his shaft.

"Holy fucking shit," burst from his mouth.

She felt incredible. He hadn't had unprotected sex since high school. With good reason.

But he wasn't going to think about that now.

Tiana began to rock her hips, and he quickly slammed his hands down on her thighs.

"Babe, you're killing me."

"So, you're saying I could fuck you to death?"

He laughed painfully. "*La petite mort.*"

Her eyebrows shot up.

"The little death." He chuckled. "Aka orgasm."

Tiana grinned and leaned over to kiss him. "And what a way to die."

"And I want this." He looked down at what he could see of her gorgeous, naked body. "But I want you to be safe. I want the—"

She kissed him again. "Don't say it," she said, her lips still touching his.

"Okay, I won't."

She sat up. "Let me ask you a question."

"Go ahead."

"Have you ever been tested? Or do you only care about your pregnant partners?"

He scowled. "Of course I have. I get tested every year when I get my physical. What do you take me for, a monster?"

A sly grin spread across her face. "No, I don't. But I wanted to show you that you're not a monster either."

She did have a point, but it had been about six months since he saw his doctor.

"Besides, I was tested for everything you can think of— standard pregnancy practice—and I came back clean." She narrowed her eyes. "Now, forget about the condom and fuck me already."

Ty laughed as he flipped her over. "What the lady wants, the lady gets."

"Yes," she hissed as he pulled out and pushed back inside her.

He was going to make them both happy and enjoy riding her with nothing between them.

But he'd still make an appointment the next day even

though he'd never skipped a condom now that he was a responsible adult because he didn't want anything to hurt her or the baby. After all, obviously, condoms sometimes failed, and the two of them were too important.

Sometime later, after both of them were well and completely satisfied, Tiana lay in his arms as he stroked his finger up and down her arm.

"I'm sorry for earlier. At the hospital. When I told everyone that you'd moved in with me. It never occurred to me that you'd keep it a secret." Ty often thought of her as mature for her age, but it was instances like this where he could see her youth.

She shrugged against his shoulder. "I wasn't planning on it." She looked up at him. "Truly." She moved her eyes back down. "It just happened so fast. I haven't seen my family since you asked me to move in, and I guess I figured I should tell them in person." She collapsed onto her back. "Now, I realize that if I'd moved in with anyone else, I wouldn't have thought the news would have to be so formal." She rolled her eyes and shook her head. "I'm not the best secret-keeper."

Ty curled onto his side and propped his head up on his hand. "I know it's hard. Do you think maybe we should tell your brother soon?"

She whipped her head toward him. "No way. Not yet. He just had his baby, and Piper needs all the support she can get right now. I don't need him mad at you and worried about me when his focus should be on his family."

And just like that, thoughts of her being young flew out the window.

She gave him a look. "Why are you smiling?"

"I was just thinking of how wise you are."

She snorted and turned away from him. "I doubt that. Otherwise, I wouldn't be in this predicament, now would I?"

He snaked an arm around her and pulled her toward him. "What predicament would that be? Pregnant or in my bed?" He kissed her shoulder. "Should I be insulted?"

Tiana chuckled. "No, you shouldn't be insulted. I like being in your bed."

"Good. Because I like you being here. And you wouldn't be here without the pregnancy, now would you?"

"Now, who's being wise? And you never know. I could have chased after you even if I wasn't pregnant."

It was Ty's turn to snort. "I doubt that."

"Oh?"

"You're the chasee, not the chaser."

"You think quite highly of me. No wonder you like me in your bed."

Ty buried his face in her naturally dark curls and laughed.

She turned in his arms. "All joking aside, I don't think it's time yet to tell everyone about the baby. We have a few months before I really start to show. And even then, it'll be winter. I'll be able to wear layers."

He kissed her cheek. "I understand. And you're right about your brother. Now's not the right time. But please remember not to keep it any more complicated than it has to be. The truth is easier to remember. And we only have to hide the baby."

"And the fact that we just had sex."

Ty grinned. "Yeah, that, too. That's one thing nobody needs to know about, including your brother."

"Even though the two secrets are kind of tied together?"

"Only the first time. Everything else is between you and me. They can all fuck off."

Tiana kissed him. "I like the way you think."

CHAPTER NINETEEN

Tiana finished turning on her computer at work and went to check her phone while it started. Only she didn't see it on her desk.

She'd gotten to work early that morning, so she'd had breakfast with her coworkers after putting her stuff away. Sometimes, she put it out of plain sight.

She opened the middle drawer in front of her. Empty. Figuring she'd forgotten to take it out of her purse, she opened the bottom drawer and searched her bag. It wasn't there either.

"What's wrong?" Alicia asked.

Tiana pulled her purse out to do a more thorough search. "I can't find my phone."

"Are you sure you brought it to work?"

She paused and did some backtracking in her mind. "Yes, because my brother sent me that text about Wyatt's party this weekend. The panicked one where he said he'd forgotten all about the cake."

Nate and Piper were having a party at their house, so everyone could meet the new baby since he'd been home for almost two weeks now.

"Uh...that was yesterday," Alicia said.

Tiana frowned. "No, it wasn't."

Alicia chuckled. "Yes, it was. You got the text right after lunch. After I spilled my drink all over the table."

"Oh my God, that was yesterday. I was thinking it was this morning." Tiana's handbag slipped from her fingers and dropped to the floor. "What's wrong with me?"

"Pregnancy brain."

She turned to her coworker. "Huh?"

"Pregnancy brain. It makes you forget everything. I knew someone who tried to shut off the faucet with her light switch."

Tiana groaned. "Why do women get pregnant again? Because we totally get screwed on this deal."

Alicia just laughed as an answer to the rhetorical question.

"I really need it today, too. I promised my brother I'd do a couple of things for Wyatt's party, so Piper wouldn't have to. And all my info is in there."

"Sorry, Ti."

Tiana looked at the clock on her computer and brightened. She might be able to catch Ty at home before he went to work. He'd gotten up early and gone to the gym, but he usually went back home before going to work since it was so close to the house. Maybe he could bring it to her.

She picked up her work phone, only to realize she didn't

have Ty's number memorized. So, she called her brother instead.

"Hello?"

"Hey, Nate."

"What's wrong?"

She thought back to Ty's advice about sticking to the truth as much as possible.

"It's not something with the party, is it?" Nate asked as worry creeped into his voice.

"Not really. I need to do a few things today for it, but I forgot my phone. Can you give me Ty's number, so I can ask him to bring it on his way to work?"

"I'll do it. I know the garage code."

An image flashed in Tiana's mind—her phone on Ty's nightstand. There was no way she could let her brother go and get it for her. She'd never be able to explain that.

Keeping her voice light and casual, she said, "No, it's fine. I'm sure Ty would be more than happy to bring it to me."

"Really, Ti, it's not a big deal."

"But you have enough stuff to do," she said, losing her will to keep a smile on her face.

"Hold on."

In the background, she could hear footsteps and then a door closing.

"Look," Nate said in a whisper, "I am going nuts over here. Paternity leave is sucking my will to live. I need something to do besides change diapers or hold the baby. I love Wyatt, but please, please let me go get your phone for you. I need to get out of this house."

Think, think, Tiana. Think of an excuse.

It was like crickets.

Stupid pregnancy brain!

"Tiana? Are you still there?"

"Yes, sorry. I'm at work, and someone was asking me a question."

What the hell? Oh, sure, now, I can think up a quick excuse.

"Well then, I won't keep you. I'll run to get your phone and bring it to you."

"Uh..."

"Oh, and where's the phone?"

"On the nightstand."

What the hell, Tiana? Way to go, you big dummy.

"Thanks, sis. I owe you."

And then Nate was gone before she could think of anything else to say to him.

"I'm so screwed," she said, setting the receiver back in its cradle.

"What's wrong?" Alicia asked.

Tiana turned to her friend. "My brother is going to go and get my phone for me."

"Ah, that's so sweet of him."

Tiana slowly shook her head. "You don't understand. I'm pretty sure that my phone is still sitting on *Ty's* nightstand."

"Oh shit."

"Exactly."

"Are you *sure*, sure? Or are you sure like you thought you got your brother's text this morning?"

"I'm ninety-nine percent sure." She'd woken up early that morning, and since she hadn't had to get out of bed yet, she'd scrolled through Instagram instead. And then she'd set it back down before getting ready for the day.

Alicia snapped her fingers. "I know. Log on to your phone account and look at your past numbers. I bet you can figure out which one is Ty's."

"Oh my God, you're a genius."

Ty was pulling out of the driveway when his phone rang. He looked at his dash where he had his cell mounted and saw that it was an unknown number.

He didn't know who it was. They could leave a message.

"Damn it, Ty, answer. I need you to answer," Tiana practically yelled into the phone.

It went to voice mail, and she hung up with a sigh.

"Call back. If he sees the number more than once, maybe he'll know it's important."

Tiana looked at Alicia. "I hope you're right."

Ty's phone rang again, and he saw that it was the same number.

"This'd better be serious," he thought out loud.

If it was a solicitor, he was hanging up on them.

"Hello?"

"Ty?"

He frowned. "Yeah? Tiana?"

"Oh, thank God. Please tell me you're still at home."

"I'm about a block away. Why?"

"I forgot my phone this morning, I didn't have your number, so I called Nate to get it, but instead, he insisted on going to pick it up himself, but when he asked, I said it was on the nightstand, except I left my phone on *your* nightstand, and if Nate finds out, he's going to kill us," Tiana said in one long sentence.

"Shit."

"Exactly. You have to go back and move it."

Ty had already turned into a driveway to head back home. "I'm on it."

"Thank you!"

"I'll call you back. Is this number good?"

"Yes."

"I'll let you know," he said and hung up the phone. He threw it on this passenger seat as he pulled into his driveway.

He barely turned off the engine before he jumped out and ran into the house and up to his room.

His eyes immediately landed on Tiana's phone. He snatched it up and sprinted for her bedroom. He dropped it on her nightstand and paused to scan the room. It looked too neat.

Ty pulled one side of the covers of the bed down and got on the mattress. He rolled around to make it look like someone had slept there and that there was a nice dent in the pillow.

He sat up and pushed the pillow on the other side off the bed. He stood and studied his work.

That's better. But he grabbed some clothes out of the closet and threw them on the bed for good measure.

He smiled, satisfied with his work and headed back for his car.

He walked outside when he heard his name being called, "Ty."

Quickly putting a surprised look on his face, he said, "Hey. What are you doing here?"

Nate rolled his eyes. "Tiana forgot her phone. I'm going to take it to her."

"Oh? That's nice of you. I would have taken it if I had known."

Nate smiled, but there was a sharpness to his look. "It's a good thing you didn't know because it's in her bedroom."

"Right." Ty stepped aside. "I'll let you go get it then."

As Nate walked into the house, Ty's heart began to race. He knew he had nothing to worry about. He'd just been inside to make sure. But he was still nervous that he'd missed something.

A minute later, Nate stepped out, shaking Tiana's phone in his hand. "I got it."

"Oh, good," he answered, his voice perhaps a little higher than usual.

They walked out of the garage as Nate said, "Man, my sister is kind of a slob." He shook his head in surprise. "I'm shocked because Trish always made her keep her room clean and her bed made."

Ty winced. He should have known that. His bed was

made every morning if Tiana got up last. And she still used her closet in the guest bedroom without leaving clothes out. He was an idiot.

"Well, I'll see you tomorrow," Nate said as he reached his car. "I'd better get this to my sister."

"Tomorrow?"

Nate turned, eyebrows raised. "Yeah. Wyatt's party."

"Oh. Right."

Nate shook his head. "You're kind of off today. You okay?"

Ty laughed awkwardly. "Yeah. It's Friday, ya know. I think my brain's already on vacation."

Nate stared off into the sky. "I'd gladly trade you."

At least, that was what Ty thought he'd said. "What?"

Nate looked back at him. "Nothing." He smiled. "See you tomorrow."

"Tomorrow."

CHAPTER TWENTY

Tiana carried Wyatt's balloons into Nate and Piper's house and held the door, so Ty could bring in Wyatt's cake.

She felt weird about not bringing in a gift, but Piper and Nate had insisted on no presents. Piper had already had a baby shower and didn't need any more presents. They wanted people to come and enjoy themselves. But part of Tiana wondered if they were just saying that, and she was going to be a shitty aunt for not getting Wyatt anything.

"Hey, there you are," Piper said.

"Where would you like everything?" Tiana asked.

"We were thinking the kitchen table would be good."

"Balloons, too?"

"Yes."

"All right," Tiana said, heading for the kitchen as Ty followed behind her. "Is there anyone else here yet?" she asked Piper as she walked.

"No. You two are the first to arrive," Piper said, following them. "Nate's changing Wyatt's diaper. They of them should be out here soon."

"Or we could be here now," Nate said from behind Piper.

Tiana practically threw the balloons down on the table, spun around, and held out her arms. "Gimme. I want to hold the baby."

Nate put Wyatt in her arms. "He's all yours." He put his arm around Piper. "And if you'll excuse us, we're going to have some alone time while you watch the baby."

Ty chuckled behind Tiana.

Piper smacked her husband in the gut. "We're doing no such thing. We have a party to finish setting up for." She turned to Nate and whispered, "You still have four weeks to wait anyway," but Tiana still heard what she'd said.

He shrugged. "There's always blow jobs."

Piper smiled a little too sweetly. "There's always your hand and the couch."

"Fine. I'll go set up the extra chairs in the living room." Nate stomped away like a little boy who'd been told he couldn't have ice cream.

Tiana smiled at her sister-in-law. "You're my idol."

"Ha. It's not that hard. Men only want one thing." She looked at Ty. "No offense."

Ty held up his hands in defeat.

"You control the sex, you control the man," Piper finished. She leaned closer to Tiana and lowered her voice. "Don't tell anyone, but I miss sex a little, too."

Tiana smiled while watching Ty out of the corner of her eye.

Then, she looked back at Piper and pretended to zip her

mouth closed. "Don't worry. I won't tell him." She gave her sister-in-law a wink.

She looked down at her nephew. "Your parents are funny."

Ty picked up the baby's foot. "I agree with your aunt." He looked up at Tiana. "I'm going to go help Nate."

Ty went downstairs to the storage room where he knew the folding chairs were kept.

"Hey," he said when he saw Nate. "How many do you need to bring upstairs?"

"I was thinking of starting with six, and if I need to bring up more, I will later."

"Hand three over to me. We can get this done in one trip."

As Nate started to move a chair over to Ty, he asked, "How's it going with my sister living with you?"

Great. Ty liked having her there more than he'd ever thought he would. They took turns making dinner and hung out together most evenings. She was fun to hang around, and he enjoyed her company. It didn't hurt that she warmed his bed every night. And after he'd gotten his all-clear from his doctor, he'd been enjoying their time together guilt-free.

He looked up at his friend. Almost guilt-free anyway.

"It's going great. She's a good roommate. She cleans up after herself, she doesn't hog all the hot water, and she hasn't thrown any wild parties."

Nate laughed and handed another chair over. "That's nice. I'm glad things are working out."

He grabbed his own chairs, and the two of them headed upstairs.

When they got to the top, they had to walk past Tiana in the kitchen.

"Ty said you're a good roommate," Nate said to his sister.

"Oh? I'm not surprised. I'm a great roommate. I'm *very* accommodating."

Ty dropped one of his chairs.

Tiana giggled.

Nate looked at Ty to see if he was okay but quickly turned back to Tiana. "I told Ty that he should make sure that you clean up your room, too," he joked.

Ty had told Tiana everything that had happened when Nate stopped over to get her phone, so she knew what her brother was talking about.

She narrowed her eyes a tad. "I'm not normally like that. But I was running late yesterday morning."

"Yeah. So late you forgot your phone."

"Exactly. Now, lay off me, Nate."

"Nope, it's my job to torment you," Nate said and headed for the living room.

"I'm sorry," Ty said as soon as Nate was out of earshot. "I really thought I was doing the right thing."

Tiana put her hand on Ty's chest. "It's fine. Really. I appreciate your attention to detail. I just wish my brother would mind his own business."

"You and me both." Ty smiled at Tiana and leaned down to kiss her.

"Mmm. What was that for?"

"For putting up with me."

Tiana grinned up at him and dropped her hand just as Piper walked back into the kitchen.

"Ty, Nate—" She stopped when she saw the two of them.

"Nate what?" Ty refused to act guilty. The two of them hadn't been doing anything when she walked in.

"He was just wondering if you were going to bring the other chairs in."

She was suspiciously looking at them, but he ignored it.

"I'm on my way."

He was barely out of the room when he heard, "Is there something going on between the two of you?"

He wanted to go back in there and rescue Tiana, but he knew that would only make them look worse.

So, he crossed his fingers for his girl and went to help Nate.

His friend grabbed the chairs and looked at Ty like he was crazy. "You okay, man? I can't tell if you're happy or afraid."

Ty shook his head. "I'm fine. Just pinched my finger, is all," he lied.

In reality, he was kind of freaking out that he'd thought of Tiana *his girl*.

He liked it, but it scared the shit out of him at the same time.

And he had no idea what to do with the information.

CHAPTER TWENTY-ONE

S everal hours had passed, and Tiana was getting tired. She'd had no idea that being around a bunch of people could wear her out. Which was why she was content to be playing in the corner with Luke and Elise's baby, Lili. She was a few months older than Wyatt, and it was crazy how different she was. She was more alert and could hold her head up for starters. She looked like she wanted to go, but she couldn't crawl yet.

"Are you two doing okay over here?"

Tiana looked up as Elise took a seat on the edge of the couch next to them.

"We're doing great, aren't we, Lili?" Tiana said.

Lili rewarded her with a sloppy grin.

"Thanks for watching her. It was nice to be baby-free for a little while," Elise said.

"No problem. I like babies. I used to babysit when I was younger."

"I have a feeling you're going to make a great mom someday."

Luke and Nate approached, and her brother snorted. "I don't think so."

This had Tiana straightening her spine. "You don't think what? That I'd be a good mom?"

Nate rolled his eyes. "I didn't mean it like that."

"Then, what did you mean?"

"I mean, you're too young. You don't even have a boyfriend."

"Oh? I didn't realize we had gone back to 1889." Tiana crossed her arms. "In case you didn't know, women have children by themselves all the time."

"Yeah, but…"

"But what?"

"But they're not you."

Tiana clenched her teeth and handed Lili over to Elise. "If you'll excuse me, I'm going to get some fresh air."

"I'll go with you," Ty said, stepping around the two other men. He held out his hand for Tiana to help her up and looked at Nate. "For the record, I think Tiana would be a great mother."

Tiana stood and straightened her clothes from sitting on the floor. "Thanks, Ty." She shot her brother a dirty look and headed for the front door. She didn't want to go out back where there would be too many people.

As soon as the door closed behind her and Ty, she said, "What an asshole."

"I don't normally say this about my friends, but I agree."

Tiana looked over her shoulder at him. "Thank you." She

chewed on her bottom lip. "You don't think he's right though, do you?"

Ty shook his head and downed the last of the soda he had been drinking. With a tilt of his head, he asked, "Do you want to get out of here?"

She really wanted to say yes. "I should stay and help clean up."

"Your parents are here. And so are Luke and Elise. I'm sure Piper and Nate can manage. Besides, right now, your brother doesn't deserve your help."

"You're not wrong about that."

"Then, let's go."

She mulled it over in her mind for a few minutes. "Okay. I need my purse though."

"You stay here. I'll go get it."

"You'd better be careful, or I'll start to think of you as a boyfriend."

The two of them froze, and Tiana wanted to slap her forehead. They might be sharing a bed every night, but they'd never even talked about dating.

And she had no idea what Ty was thinking. His expression was unreadable.

She groaned. "Forget I said that." She tried to play her words off with a laugh.

Ty winked. "I'll think about it," he said and then turned on his heel and went back inside.

Tiana pulled her phone out of her pocket.

Tiana: I just told Ty I might start to think of him as a boyfriend if he didn't stop doing nice things for me.

Jasmine: Shit, girl, you really know how to put your foot in it.

Tiana: I know. Ugh.

Jasmine: What did he say?

Tiana: Nothing. He just stared at me. Finally, I told him to forget I said it and laughed. Then, he winked and said he'd think about it.

Jasmine: He winked?

Tiana: Yes.

Jasmine: What a weirdo.

Tiana: Hey! I thought it was cute and sexy. It was definitely not weird.

Jasmine: Hahahahahahaha!

Tiana: Why are you laughing at me?

Jasmine: Because you really do think of him as boyfriend material. Look at you, all defending him and shit.

Tiana: I am not.

Jasmine: You'd better be careful, or you might fall in love with him.

Tiana: And why would that be bad?

> Jasmine: You're already having a baby. Next thing you know, you'll get married, and then you'll never get your CPA.

Tiana bit her lip. *Would that be so bad?*

> Jasmine: Just be careful, okay? I'm not saying Ty is a bad guy. But you and I know too many people who have gotten married or stayed together because they got pregnant. And someone in the relationship has to sacrifice things, and we both know it isn't generally the guy.

> Jasmine: I would hate to see you put off school, only for the two of you to break up five years from now. And by then, you might have another kid and won't want to or be able to go back to school.

Tiana wanted to tell Jasmine she was wrong, but that had happened to a couple of girls they knew from high school. The patriarchy was still alive, and...well, it was usually the woman who got screwed.

When Tiana didn't text back, Jasmine sent another message.

> Jasmine: Look, I'm not saying you can't have fun with him or even start a relationship, but please make sure you're not the only one making sacrifices.

> Tiana: Ty's not like that.

> Jasmine: Yeah. He's not like that until he is.

Tiana: He's really not. But I promise to keep a clear head, okay?

Jasmine: That's all I ask.

"Everything okay?" Ty asked as he came outside with her purse.

"Yes. My best friend is just having some guy troubles, is all."

She felt bad for lying, but there was not a chance in hell she was going to tell Ty that they had been texting about him.

"Sorry to hear that."

Tiana shrugged. "I'm sure it'll all work out."

Ty's eyes widened at her nonchalant comment, but she didn't have the energy to pretend to care about Jasmine's nonexistent man.

"Where are we going?" she asked, changing the subject.

The two of them walked down the stone steps to Ty's car.

"I was thinking that you deserved a date."

"A date?" Jasmine's words about sacrifices rang in her head, but Tiana couldn't help but be excited.

"Yes. You've been spending every night with me, and we mostly sit at home. I have yet to take you out." He smiled. "And it's just not right." He cocked an eyebrow. "How does that sound to you?"

Tiana tapped her chin as she pretended to think about it. She dropped her hand and grinned. "I'm game. On one condition."

"What's that?"

"That we go somewhere far from here so that we don't run into anyone we know. If we're going on a date, I want it to be a real date. No secretly holding hands or anything like that."

"I like the sound of that." He grimaced. "We might have to drive a ways."

She waved her hand. "Doesn't bother me." She looked at her phone. "It's only four in the afternoon anyway. We have plenty of time."

"Sounds like a plan." Ty started walking over to her side of the car.

She put her hand up. "What are you doing?"

"Opening the door for you. If it's a date, don't you think we should do it properly?"

She laughed. "I appreciate it, but it's not needed. I can open my own door, thank you very much. Plus, we don't know who's watching out the window."

"Oh. Right. Good call."

Ty hit the unlock button on his key fob, and they got into their seats.

"I am going to open the door for you at least once," he warned her with a grin and started his car.

Tiana knew he was just being a gentleman, but the old-fashioned thinking along with Jasmine's words made her feel a little uneasy.

She looked at Ty's profile. No matter how nice he was and how much she liked him, she could not—would not—sacrifice her future for him.

CHAPTER TWENTY-TWO

Ty drummed his fingers on the steering wheel, trying to think of something that he and Tiana could do for entertainment that night. He wanted to do something besides just go out to dinner but nothing like hitting up a club, as it might not be as much fun since she couldn't drink. Plus, he wasn't sure if loud music was good for the baby.

He was just about to ask if Tiana had any ideas when his phone buzzed, and a message popped up from Ethan, a coworker of his and Nate's.

> Ethan: How was the party? Was Kayla there?

Kayla and Ethan had dated and broken up, but he still had a thing for her.

But this gave Ty an idea.

He grabbed his phone and handed it to Tiana. "Will you text Ethan back for me since I'm driving?"

She gave him an odd look but agreed.

She thrust it back at him. "I need you to unlock it."

"The code is zero-five-eight-three." When he didn't see any movement out of the corner of his eye, he quickly glanced at her. "What's wrong?"

She smiled, her eyes turned down, and shook her head. "Nothing." She put in his code and said, "What do you want me to text?"

"Tell him, yes, Kayla was there, and then ask him if he still has his tickets to the comedy club tonight."

He could see Tiana's thumbs moving, and then she put the phone in her lap. "Why did he ask about Kayla?"

"Do you know who she is?"

"I've met her once or twice. She was at the wedding. And I said hello to her today." She turned in her seat toward him. "Is Ethan the guy with the red hair? He was at the wedding, too, right?"

"Yep, that's him."

"Why wasn't he at Wyatt's party today?"

"He's sick, which is why he can't go to the comedy club tonight. He and Kayla dated for quite a few months but broke up after the wedding." Ty glanced at Tiana. "He's still heartbroken over her, although he'd never admit it."

"Why'd they break up?"

Ty shrugged. "I don't really know. Ethan won't say, and neither Nate nor I have pushed the issue."

His phone buzzed in her lap.

"What did he say?"

She unlocked his phone again. "He says he still has the tickets and wants to know why you're asking."

"Tell him I want them if I can still have them."

Quick movements of her thumbs. "Done. He also asked if Kayla was alone. I told him yes."

"Thank you."

Buzz.

"He says the tickets are yours."

"Tell him we'll be there in twenty minutes." He looked over at her. "Unless you're not up for it."

"Is it the comedy club that also has a restaurant?"

He grinned. "That's the one. I thought we could eat and catch the show after."

"I've heard good things about the place. I've always wanted to go." She smiled at him. "Let's do it."

Ty loved watching Tiana smile. Her laugh was infectious. He caught himself laughing more because she was laughing than because he thought the comedian was funny.

The starting comic just finished his set before the headliner came out, and the room grew a lot quieter. People around them were getting up to stretch, use the restrooms, and refill their drinks.

Tiana scooted nearer to him and snuggled close. "Thanks for bringing me here."

He turned toward her, and his mouth brushed her forehead, so he rubbed his nose against her temple and leaned next to her ear. "You're having a good time then?"

"Mmhmm," she said, her voice taking on a sultry tone.

Ty had to reach under the tablecloth and adjust himself. He looked at his watch. "Is it time to leave yet?" he joked.

Tiana slid her hand past his belt buckle and over his swollen shaft. "I wish," she whispered in his ear.

He squirmed in his seat and scanned the room. They were toward the back, where it was dark, and no one was paying them any attention, so he closed his eyes and enjoyed her touch for a minute.

Feeling like he might hit the point of no return, he put his hand over hers and looked at her. "You have to stop now."

"Why's that?"

He chuckled. "Because I'm going to come in my pants if you don't. When I walk out of here, everyone is going to think that I either blew my load or wet myself. I'm not sure which is worse."

Tiana met his eyes. "Do you trust me?"

"Uh...yes." He had no idea how she meant that question, but it didn't matter because he trusted her.

She picked up his hand and set it on the table. "Then, let me do what I need to do." She kissed him. "And I promise no one will think anything about you when you walk out of here." The corner of her mouth curled up. "Except maybe how happy you look."

"If you say so."

"Oh, I know so, baby."

She slid her hand back down toward his crotch again, but this time, she unbuttoned his pants and slipped her hand in his boxers. Her warm fingers curled around his aching dick.

Ty hissed, and his breath caught.

"Just keep your eyes on the stage, and no one will even

know what I'm doing to you," Tiana advised him as she gently stroked him.

"That's going to be hard, but I'll try."

She snickered.

"No pun intended." His last word came out as a squeak as she squeezed him. "*Merde*."

"Why are you always cursing in French when we fuck?"

"Because I was born there. I moved to the US when I was little."

"That's right. I think I knew that. There's so much more I need to learn about you."

"I'm not sure if now is the time."

Ty was getting close to orgasm, and holding a conversation was getting more difficult. He started to turn his head toward Tiana, but she stopped him with a nip on the ear.

"Uh-uh-uh. Keep facing forward."

"But I'm going to—"

"Shh...it's okay. I've got you." She kissed his cheek as she continued to caress him. "You trust me, remember?"

He nodded because words were beyond him now.

Ty was doing everything he could to keep his climax at bay when Tiana moved her arm and knocked her purse off the table.

"Oops. I'd better get that before I lose my stuff on the floor."

Before he could say anything, Tiana let his erection go and disappeared under the table.

Two seconds later, her hand was back, and her mouth wrapped around his dick. Unprepared for the impromptu blow job, he took less than a minute to explode into her mouth.

And Tiana was right. As the two of them walked out of the club after the head comedian was done an hour later, Ty was grinning like a fool.

CHAPTER TWENTY-THREE

The next morning, Tiana lay in bed, too sleepy to get up yet. It was Sunday, so there was no rush to get ready for work.

Her phone rang. She didn't even look to see who was calling before she answered since she didn't want it to wake Ty.

But after she swiped the green button, she wished she'd just muted the call because it was Nate.

"Hello?"

"Did I wake you up?"

"No."

"You sound like it."

"I've been up. I just haven't said anything yet, so my voice is still hoarse. Thanks for asking."

"Sorry. I didn't mean to offend you."

And typically, she probably wouldn't have been, but she was still upset about what he'd said the day before.

Ty rolled over in his sleep and muttered something unintelligible.

"Was that Ty?" Nate asked.

Tiana took a deep breath and told herself not to get nervous. She pushed back the covers and got up as she said, "No. Just the TV."

"Oh. I could have sworn it sounded like Ty. You're not sleeping with him, are you?" Her brother laughed at his joke.

Tiana sighed and headed for the kitchen. "What do you want, Nate? I haven't had my coffee yet this morning, and I'm not in the mood for you right now."

"Ouch."

Normally, she'd care about his feelings more, but she hadn't been lying about the coffee.

She shrugged. "If the shoe fits."

This time, he sighed. "I called to tell you I'm sorry, okay?"

Tiana pulled out the coffee and filled the coffeemaker with water. "You called, or your wife made you call?"

"My wife encouraged me. I'd like to say it was all my decision."

"Right."

"She's not the boss of me, you know."

Tiana snorted. "Sure."

"You're a brat."

"And you're an asshole."

Nate growled into the phone. "You're making this really hard."

"That's what little sisters are for."

The reminder of their relationship seemed to calm Nate

some because his next words were, "I really am sorry. I felt bad after you left."

She slammed the top of the coffeepot down. "Yeah, well, it wasn't very nice."

Knowing the coffee would take a few minutes, she went into the living room, plopped down on the couch, and turned on the television.

"I know I wasn't nice," her brother said. "That's why I'm apologizing."

"Then, why did you say it?" She looked down at her abdomen. "Do you really think I'd be a bad mother?"

"*No*. In fact, Piper and I want you to babysit."

"So, that's why you called me."

"Not today, you brat. I mean, sometime in the future. Date unknown."

"I know, Nate. I was teasing you."

"Does that mean you forgive me?"

"Not yet."

"What?"

"Explain more. What did you mean when you said I was too young and didn't even have a boyfriend? You think I can't do it on my own?"

"No, that's not it at all."

"Then, what is it?"

"I don't want you to *have* to do it on your own. I know you want to go back to school. And I want you to have what Piper and I have. I want your baby to be made with someone you love."

Tiana made a gagging noise.

Nate tsked. "Make fun of me all you want. I only want

you to be happy," he said, the tone of his voice making him sound frustrated with her.

"I'm sorry for teasing. But you're very sweet."

"Shh. Don't tell anyone."

"Your wife probably already knows."

"No, she's with me because she knows what a stallion I am."

"Oh, gross. I need to go and puke."

The two of them were laughing at each other when she heard the steps creak behind her.

She looked over her shoulder to see a sleepy Ty walking down the stairs. He looked at her phone as he came closer.

Nate, she mouthed.

You okay?

She nodded and smiled. *He apologized.*

Good.

The coffeemaker beeped, and Ty walked into the kitchen. A minute later, he came back with a cup of coffee while she continued talking to Nate.

She pulled her phone away from her mouth. "Is that for me?" she whispered, pointing to the mug.

Ty took a sip, grinned, and shook his head.

"Why not?" she whispered as Nate continued prattling on about his new son.

"Because I have something else for you," he said in a low voice.

She raised her eyebrows. *That sounds ominous.*

Ty set his coffee down on the end table and got to his knees. She simply watched, curious as to what he was going to do next.

When he reached for the waistband of her pajamas, she widened her eyes. "What are you doing?" she hissed.

Ty smirked. "I'm paying you back."

He whipped off her bottoms and pushed her legs wide. "Mmm...morning pussy," he said.

She snapped her legs closed.

He looked up at her and frowned.

"I need to shower first," she said in a normal voice. She'd completely forgotten she was still on the phone with her brother.

"Why do you need to shower before I take Wyatt on a walk?" Nate's voice sounded full of confusion. "Did you want to go with?"

"What?" She had no idea what he'd been talking about.

"You just said you needed to shower. I was asking..."

Tiana tuned Nate out as she watched Ty lower his head between her legs. *When did they open back up?*

She really needed to choose to concentrate on one thing.

"Nate, I have to go," she interrupted him.

"But you didn't even—"

"Talk to you later. Bye." She made sure the phone was disconnected and threw it on the couch as Ty hit a particularly sensitive spot on her. "Oh, yeah. That feels amazing."

He lifted his head. "You were supposed to stay on the phone."

"It was my brother," she pointed out.

"And I was in a room full of strangers last night."

She laughed. "Not the same thing. You could have sex with those strangers."

"Fair point. I really wanted to torture you though."

She crooked her finger at him, and he inched forward on his knees. Wrapping her arms around his neck, she told him, "Just make love to me real slow, like until I'm begging to come. That'll show me."

Ty wasn't impressed. "Nice try. I know you'd like that. How about, instead, I give you a quickie and leave you hanging?"

She gasped. "You wouldn't?"

Ty lifted her hips and settled her right over his hard length. "You're right. I wouldn't. I like watching you come way too much."

CHAPTER TWENTY-FOUR

Ty rotated Tiana's body under his so that they could lie lengthwise on the couch. Screwing on the couch in a sitting position reminded him of being in high school, sneaking around, and having sex in the backseat because there was nowhere else to go.

He wasn't a teenager anymore, and he could fuck anywhere he wanted. It was his house.

He grinned and pushed Tiana's hands over the side of the couch.

"Why are you so happy?" Tiana asked him.

He left her arms where he'd laid them and unbuttoned her pajama top. He sighed when he pushed the sides apart and her breasts were exposed. Her dark nipples peaked to attention as the cool air hit them.

Ty smiled and sucked one nipple into his mouth. "Mmm...you taste good."

Before she could answer, he slid down and out of her body.

She lifted her head. "What are you doing?"

"Finishing what I started," he told her, putting one of her legs on the back of the couch and her other foot on the floor. "Nice," he said at the view in front of him.

Ty licked the seam of her pussy up to her clit. But instead of putting it in his mouth, he circled it with his tongue and headed back the way he'd come. He pulled each lip of her vagina into his mouth and then shoved his tongue into her.

When she started humping his face, he finally made his way back to her sensitive nub and pushed the flat of his tongue against it.

Tiana squirmed under him, and he fought a smile. He loved making her feel good.

He lightly teased her opening with two fingers before gently pressing them inside her and up to her G-spot.

When she was close to orgasm, he pulled his hand away and moved his mouth from her clit, starting all over in making love to her pussy with his lips and tongue.

He did this three times as Tiana moaned, whimpered, and cried out.

Finally, she must have had enough because she clasped the sides of his head with both hands and said, "Why are you doing this to me?"

He played innocent. "You suggested I tease you until you begged to come."

"I said, make love, not tease."

He shrugged. "Semantics."

"You're evil."

Despite the hold she had on him, Ty leaned down and swiped his tongue over her clit.

She groaned.

He lifted his head back up. "I'm still waiting for you to beg me."

"Can't you tell by all the noises I'm making that I'm going crazy?"

Ty kissed her vagina. Just a peck. "No." He shook his head. "I want to hear the words. I want to hear that I'm making you crazy. I want to hear you beg to come."

She smiled and shook her head. "Never."

"Okay." Ty got up on his knees and was ready to leave the couch. He was calling her bluff and hoped she caved because he felt like his dick was going to explode.

She sprang into a sitting position and grabbed his sides. "Don't go."

Ty kissed her neck. "Why not?"

"Because you can't leave me like this."

He smiled into her neck. "Oh?"

He slowly laid her back down and kissed his way down her body again. He kissed her pelvic bone and the inside of both thighs. He pried her lips apart and blew air onto her swollen nub.

"You win. Please, please, please make me come. I need it so bad."

"The pleasure is all mine." Ty pushed his fingers inside her again and sucked her clit into his mouth.

Within seconds, she was all but dripping on his fingers and crying out in pleasure. He did his best to make sure her orgasm was nice and long before he crawled back up her body and gently pressed himself inside her.

She hissed.

"You okay?" He knew he wasn't small, but he was surprised since he felt like he had prepared her.

She looked him in the eye. "Perfectly okay." She ran her hands up his arms. "I'm so sensitive; it's as if I can feel every centimeter of you."

He leaned down and kissed her. "I love the sound of that."

She wrapped her arms around his neck and pulled his lips back to hers. She licked into his mouth, and he was surprised. Most women he'd been with didn't want to taste themselves.

He found it incredibly hot that Tiana didn't shy away from it.

He began to pump his hips and pulled away enough to look down on her. "Do you like the way you taste on me?"

She ran her tongue over her lips. "I do."

"That is so sexy."

She grinned. "Maybe I'll show you just how much when I take you in my mouth after you come in me."

Ty's dick twitched, and he almost came. "Holy shit." He pounded into her harder now, lifting up her leg and pushing it to her shoulder. He wanted to be as deep as possible. "You know how to flip a guy's sex switch."

She laughed against his ear and said, "It's only fair since you flip mine. Now, will you please make me come again? I want to feel you explode in me."

Ty thrust into Tiana, holding on long enough to make her climax again before he let his orgasm take hold of his body and wash over him.

The two of them lay there for a few seconds, breathing

hard and regaining the ability to think. At least, that was what Ty was doing.

Tiana pushed at his shoulder, and he suddenly remembered that he was heavy and most likely squishing her and the baby.

"Shit. Sorry." He scrambled off her and sat on the couch.

Tiana's leg was behind his head, so he helped her bring it down as she sat up, too. She leaned toward him, and he couldn't help but notice her beautiful breasts peeking out from her open PJs.

He lifted a hand and thumbed her nipple.

"Ty?"

"Hmm?" he said and looked up at her.

"I can't do my thing if you keep staring at my boobs."

His brow furrowed. "Your thing?"

She chuckled and bent over to his lap. Just as she'd said, she sucked him into her mouth, and Ty nearly came out of his seat.

"Holy fuck. *Merde*. Damn it."

She licked him clean before carefully releasing him from her hold.

He was so spent that he couldn't lift his head from the back of the couch where it had fallen.

She snuggled closer and kissed his cheek before putting her mouth on his.

Wanting to show her he was as sexually adventurous as her, he cupped the back of her head and kissed her deeply. He tasted both of them on her tongue, and he liked it.

When she pulled away, he smiled at her. "You are amazing."

"So are you," she told him.

He put his arm around her and held her for a bit. Feeling like he might doze off, he asked her, "Do you want to shower first, or do you want me to?"

He had two showers, but there was always more hot water if they didn't take them at the same time.

"Can't we lie here for a little while longer?"

"Sorry, babe. We can't. We have to see my parents today."

"That's right." She moved from his side. "Go shower then. I don't want you to smell like sex when they meet me."

He laughed, but deep inside, he agreed. The two of them had decided that she should meet his parents as a casual roommate first before they told them that they were going to be grandparents.

His parents had met Nate but not his sister, and Ty wanted to make sure they liked her for her and not because she was having his baby.

Ty got up from the couch and went into the kitchen.

"I thought you were going to go shower," she called out.

"I am," he called back. "I just need to get something first."

"What's that?" she asked as he walked back in, carrying a cup of coffee.

He set the new cup down and picked up the old one.

She watched him but didn't say anything.

He turned toward the stairs. "I'll let you know when I'm out."

"You forgot your other cup of coffee."

"No, I didn't. That one's for you."

CHAPTER TWENTY-FIVE

Tiana smiled to herself as she sipped her coffee and relaxed on the couch in post-coital bliss. It was such a little thing, for him to bring her coffee, but she secretly loved it.

She'd just put her feet up and found something to watch on TV when the doorbell rang.

She looked at the clock on the wall. It wasn't quite eleven in the morning yet. Ty's parents were scheduled to be there at twelve to twelve thirty, so it couldn't be them.

She suddenly remembered the phone call with her brother and groaned. She hoped that Nate hadn't driven over. She honestly couldn't recall everything that they'd talked about, but she knew there was some confusion at the end.

She momentarily panicked and checked her clothes and hair but remembered that she was still in her pajamas, so it was okay if she looked like she'd been sleeping. She just hoped she didn't smell like sex.

She quickly ran into the kitchen and lit a candle she'd bought for the house when the doorbell rang again.

"I'm coming," she called out in her best calm voice.

Fully expecting to see her brother on the other side of the door, she didn't even look before she opened it.

But it wasn't her brother standing there. It was an older couple she had never seen before.

Crap.

They had to be Ty's parents. And she looked awful.

Oh no. This was not how she'd wanted to make a first impression.

"Is Ty home, young lady?" Ty's father asked with raised eyebrows when she didn't say anything.

"Oh, yes. I'm sorry. Please, come in." She stepped back, so they could enter, and she caught a whiff of her breath. She clamped her lips shut, closed the door, and stepped far, far away from them before she spoke again, "I'll just go and tell Ty that you're here."

She turned and ran up the stairs and into Ty's room.

He was just coming out of the shower when she burst in and slammed his door closed.

"What's wrong?"

"Your parents are here."

He laughed. "That's not so bad. When I saw the look on your face, I thought maybe something horrible had happened."

She threw her hands up. "Something bad did happen." She pulled at her clothes. "I'm in my pajamas. I have bedhead-slash-just-been-fucked hair. I didn't greet them at the door. I have a combination of morning, dick, vagina, and coffee breath. And I didn't offer them anything to eat or even ask them to sit down while I came upstairs to get you."

She'd been slowly stalking closer to Ty as she whisper-ranted, and he put his hands on her shoulders.

"It'll be okay. I promise. My parents are cool."

She stepped back and fell against his bed. "Doesn't matter. I'm not going back down there."

He chuckled. "And what am I going to tell them happened to you?"

She flung a hand over her eyes. "Tell them I died."

Ty burst out laughing. "I don't think they'd believe it. Besides, they're really not that scary." He pulled her arm away. "Go and get ready. Take your time. We're not supposed to go to lunch for at least an hour. And when we do, you'll see that you had nothing to worry about."

Tiana hurried to get ready, and then she casually walked downstairs to officially meet Ty's parents. She didn't want them to think she was nervous or anything.

The three of them looked up from where they were seated around the living room as she got to the bottom of the stairs.

Ty stood and walked over to her. "Mom, Dad, this is Tiana Hall. She's Nate Hall's sister. Tiana, this is my mother and father, Cleo and Hudson Morgan."

"Hello," Tiana said to them both.

Tiana's father smiled at her. "It's nice to meet you. You're Nate's little sister? Your brother is a good guy."

Ty put a hand on the small of her back and nudged her toward the middle of the room—she guessed to go sit down with his parents. It was a minor move, but she noticed Ty's mother had zeroed in on it right away. And she didn't look happy.

Oh no, we're not off to a good start.

Tiana sat down in one of the recliners and tried not to blush at the vision of Ty's parents sitting on the couch. She might have darker skin, but her cheeks still lit up like a Christmas tree when she reddened.

"I'm sorry I ran out of here earlier. I had just woken up not too long before you arrived, and I hadn't had a chance to get ready yet."

Nate's mother looked at her. "Did Tyler not tell you when we were coming?" she asked in a light French accent.

The accent wasn't what threw Tiana off. It was hearing Ty being called by his full name. It made her think of another person, so it took a second or two for her to answer, "Oh, um, yes. Ty said that you were coming around noon. I thought we still had an hour."

"One must always be prepared," his mom said.

"Mom, we were up late last night, and we both woke up just a little bit ago."

His mother looked at the both of them with criticism in her eyes. "Young women should not be out drinking late."

"Cleo," Ty's father said in a warning tone.

"I apologize, but it is how I feel."

Tiana would eat her shirt if the lady was even ten percent sorry for what she'd said. It was bullshit. She didn't like Tiana and wanted Tiana to know it.

"We actually went to a comedy club last night, Mom. Tiana didn't have anything to drink."

Tiana shot Ty a thank-you look for sticking up for her.

Ty's mom made a disapproving noise.

Ty's father must have decided it was time to change the subject. "How long have you been living with Ty?"

"A few weeks. He was kind enough to let me move in after my last roommate made a sudden adjustment in her living arrangements."

"Do you have a job?" Ty's mom asked.

Wow. This lady is something.

"Yes. I work at a bank in the accounting department. I'm saving up money so that I can get my master's."

Maybe it was because there was not a good comeback to Tiana's news, but for whatever reason, Ty's mom didn't say anything.

"That's very ambitious."

"Thank you, Mr. Morgan."

He smiled. "You can call me Hudson."

Tiana smiled back. "Thank you, Hudson."

"When do you plan to go?" Ty's mom asked.

"I'm not sure. I was looking into this fall or next spring, but we'll see, Mrs. Morgan."

"Why the change of plans?" she asked Tiana, and Tiana noticed she hadn't offered to be called by her first name.

Ty clapped his hands. "I think it's about time we head to lunch, don't you?"

Tiana welcomed the interruption. She didn't have a good excuse as to why she was waiting to go back to school. And it definitely wasn't the time to tell his parents that she was pregnant.

Tiana looked at Ty's mom. Maybe when the baby graduated high school was when they'd tell them because, right now, it felt like Mrs. Morgan was never going to like her.

"I suppose it is time we go. We don't want to be late," Ty's father said.

"I made a reservation at our favorite brunch place," Ty's mom said to him with a smile on her face.

It was official. She wasn't in a bad mood. She just didn't like Tiana.

Ty rubbed his hands together. "Ooh. I can't wait." He looked at Tiana. "Have you ever eaten—"

"I'm sorry, dear," Mrs. Morgan interrupted. "I only made reservations for three."

Ty cocked his head to the side. "Mom, I'm sure they can make room for one more. That way, we can all get to know each other better. We can't leave Tiana home alone while we go out."

"Why not? This is the first time we have even met your *roommate*. As you pointed out, we're strangers."

The ice in his mom's words was hard to miss.

She turned to Tiana. "And I'm sure you have other things you'd rather do, right, dear?" The woman smiled, but it was anything but friendly. It was a warning.

The joke was on her. Tiana had no desire to go out to eat with the horrible woman. She'd honestly rather stay home, order a pizza, and relax.

Tiana smiled the sweetest smile she could muster. "Oh, yes, I wouldn't want to intrude on your family time. I have some things I need to do before I go to work tomorrow anyway." She practically batted her eyelashes at the woman.

Mrs. Morgan didn't notice or didn't care. She turned to Ty. "See? We shall go to lunch. Just the three of us."

Ty looked at Tiana and mouthed, *I'm sorry.*

Later that night, Ty lay in bed, waiting for Tiana to come up from downstairs. Rather than shouting through the house, he grabbed his phone.

> Ty: Are you coming to bed?

> Tiana: In a bit.

Ty sighed and tapped his phone against his chest. He knew she was upset about what had happened with his mom, but she'd refused to talk about it. He'd apologized, and she'd said there was no need, but she'd been cool since he got home.

He picked up the cell again.

> Ty: I miss you.

> Tiana: How can you miss me? I'm downstairs.

> Ty: I can't go to sleep without you.

A few seconds later, he heard her footsteps. She walked through the door and put her hands on her hips.

"Last night, you were snoring before I was done brushing my teeth. I call bullshit that you can't sleep without me."

He grinned. "How about, I don't want to sleep without you?"

She didn't smile at the words that he'd thought would make her happy. Instead, she crossed the room to the bed, put her phone down on the nightstand, and sat down on the edge of the bed.

Ty sat up. "I really am sorry about my mother."

She looked over her shoulder at him. "Ty, it's fine."

"No, it's not. You're the mother of my child. She shouldn't treat you like that."

"In her defense, she doesn't know that I'm the mother of your child, does she?"

"Then, I amend my statement. She shouldn't treat you like that, no matter what."

Tiana turned sideways on the bed, so she wouldn't have to stretch her neck. "Is she always like that?"

He threw up his hands. "*No.* That's why I don't get it. And when I tried to talk to her about it, she would change the subject or blow me off."

"You tried to talk to her?"

"Of course I did, Ti. You're special to me, and I don't want to see you hurt."

She looked him in the eyes. "I appreciate it. I really do. But you're not getting laid. I'm not in the mood."

Ty burst out laughing and pulled her down to him. "I didn't do it for sex. Like I said, I care about you."

Ty waited for her to say something in return, but she was

silent. He lifted his head to see what she was thinking, only to realize that she wasn't awake.

He yanked the covers over the two of them and cuddled her close.

He was going to give her so much crap in the morning about falling asleep on him in the middle of an important conversation.

CHAPTER TWENTY-SIX

Life moved on, and before they knew it, it was the halfway mark for Tiana's pregnancy. They had their second ultrasound.

Tiana held up the pictures that the sonographer had printed off. As they walked out of the building, Tiana said, "I can't believe we're having a girl."

Ty put his arm around her. "I didn't think you'd had any hints about if it was one sex or the other."

She dropped her hands and wrinkled her nose. "That's what I thought. But when she said it was a girl, I thought she had to be wrong. Until she showed us the proof." Not that Tiana knew what she was looking at, but she trusted the professional who had said she did.

"Well, I'm just glad that the baby is healthy," Ty said.

After Tiana's ultrasound, they'd gone straight to her doctor's appointment and been given the good news.

"I know it's cliché, and everyone says it, but me, too,"

Tiana agreed. She took a deep breath. "I suppose it's time we start thinking about telling everyone, huh?"

Ty nodded his head. "I suppose. We know everything's okay, so there's no reason to hold off."

Tiana rubbed her abdomen. "And I'm going to start really showing soon." She already had a small belly, but nothing clothes couldn't hide. But she didn't know how much longer that would last.

"Yeah, and I want people to hear it from us rather than figure it out on their own."

"Ugh. This is going to be so hard. Who do we tell first?"

"And who do we tell last?"

"I always thought it would be my brother, but now, I'm leaning toward your mom. At least Nate likes you."

Ty immediately looked defeated. "I don't think she doesn't like you. She doesn't know you."

"And she doesn't want to get to know me," Tiana pointed out.

She had told Ty she was fine, but after a day or so, she had still been a little peeved at his mom's treatment of her. To be honest, she was still mad even though it had been over a week ago.

But she knew it wasn't Ty's fault, and she felt bad. He was trying.

She put her hand on his arm. "I'm sorry. I know you're going to talk to her."

"I am. I have a plan, and I don't care how awkward it's going to be," he said with a half-smile.

"You'll do fine."

"I just had a thought."

"Oh?" Tiana asked.

"What if we had everyone over and told them about the pregnancy at the same time? No one would have to be the first, and no one would have to be the last."

"Are you insane? It would be us against all of them. They could gang up on us."

"Ohh. I didn't think of it like that."

"Unless..."

"Unless what?"

"We could get them together, drop the news, and then leave." Tiana laughed as she pictured how that would go in her mind. She would never actually do it, but it was fun to think about.

"You're hilarious."

"I know."

"I was joking about telling everyone at the same time," Ty pointed out.

"I know. So was I," she said.

Ty laughed and kissed her on the forehead.

They reached his vehicle. Ty dropped his arm from around her shoulders, but neither of them got in.

"We really do need to figure out how we're going to tell everyone."

Tiana huffed out a breath. "I know. I was thinking, my parents first. Even though I think they'll be a little disappointed, I don't see them getting mad at me. But I was also thinking I should tell them on my own."

"I don't want your dad to assume I'm a coward."

"He's not going to do that. But I feel it's something I need to do alone first." Tiana leaned back against the car. "I don't know if it's the right choice. I've never done this before."

Ty moved to stand beside her. "Yeah, it sucks. Don't you hate how we're both grown adults and the situation makes us feel like we're teenagers again?"

"Yes. That is it."

He picked up her hand. "No matter what, at least you have me."

That was really sweet of Ty to say, but part of her had to wonder if he felt that way because of the baby or because he liked her that much.

With all the stress of keeping the pregnancy a secret, they'd never discussed their relationship. Sure, they lived together, and she slept in his bed every night, but they were still telling people she was his roommate.

If they were going to be more than that in the long run, wouldn't it make more sense to tell others they were dating? And when announcing the pregnancy, wouldn't it make more sense for the news to come from two people who were a couple instead of a couple of friends?

"What's wrong?" Ty asked. "You suddenly look very stressed."

She raised her eyebrows. "This is a stressful subject."

"I know, but the look on your face just got worse."

"I think just the enormity of the whole situation is catching up to me."

Ty picked up her hand and kissed the back of it. "How about we forget about it for the rest of the day? We got some good news and should celebrate. And we can tell the people who do know about the baby the good news, like your best friend."

"You're right."

"How do you want to celebrate?"

"With ice cream?"

Ty laughed. "Ice cream it is."

"And maybe start making plans for a baby shower. Even though some people aren't going to be happy at first, I think they'll come around."

Ty's eyes lit up. "Maybe that's how we tell them. We'll just invite them to the baby shower."

Tiana laughed. "That is pure evil."

"I know. It would be funny though."

CHAPTER TWENTY-SEVEN

A little less than a week later, Ty walked up to his parents' house. Monday had been the ultrasound and doctor's appointment, and it was now Saturday. Tiana was babysitting Wyatt for Nate and Piper tonight, and Ty had decided it was the perfect time to visit his mom and dad.

He'd thought he'd have to twist their arms—or rather, his mother's arm—to say yes, but she hadn't fought him at all when he suggested dinner. Her only stipulation was that he came over for dinner instead of going out.

He figured it was because she didn't want to risk him bringing Tiana along, but he hadn't bothered telling his mom that Tiana had other plans. He didn't want to start a fight before his mom had more time around Tiana again. He didn't want an argument to cloud her view of Tiana.

He knocked on the door and entered.

He had expected to see his dad sitting in front of the television while his mom finished up dinner, but instead, he walked inside to see his parents were not alone.

"Hello, Tyler, my dear boy," his mom said. She walked up to him and kissed him on the cheek. His mom was the only person who called him by his first name. She refused to call him Ty.

"Hey, Mom. What's going on?"

"You remember the Johnsons, right?"

There were three other people in the room who had to be the Johnsons. A couple about his parents' age and a woman around his.

Now, he understood why his mother had wanted him to come over for dinner.

He wanted to turn around and leave, but he'd been raised to be polite. "Hello again," he said rather than bolting out the door.

"Tyler, this is Benjamin Johnson; his wife, Francis; and their daughter, Naomi. Do you remember them?"

"Yes," Ty said. "It's been a while." He held out his hand for Benjamin to shake. "How are you doing, sir?"

Benjamin laughed. "Ben is fine. And I'm doing well."

Ty nodded to Francis and Naomi. Naomi smiled at him in sympathy.

She obviously knew it was a setup, too. She was a beautiful woman with smooth, dark skin, braids down to the middle of her back, and intelligent eyes. But to him, she wasn't as beautiful as Tiana.

That was when it hit him that he truly cared about her, and he had never even bothered to tell her.

They'd been pretty much living together as boyfriend and girlfriend, but they hadn't discussed being exclusive. And that needed to change.

"Ty, dear?" his mother said. "Are you even listening?"

He smiled apologetically. "Sorry, what did you say?"

"I said, we should all sit down, and I asked if you wanted a drink."

He held up one finger. "I'll take you up on that in one minute. I need to make a quick phone call first."

His mother shook her head. "Tyler, that is rude. You should really put your phone on silent, so it doesn't interrupt us."

"Mom, I will only be a second."

She narrowed her eyes at him.

"Fine. I'll have a glass of whatever everyone else is having." Ty pulled out his phone and turned it to vibrate.

His mother smiled. "Hudson, can you grab our son a drink?"

"Sure thing."

"Tyler, did you know that Naomi owns her own business?" his mom said to him.

Ty shook his head and braced himself for a long night.

Tiana laid a sleeping Wyatt down in the bassinet Nate and Piper kept in their room as carefully as she could. He'd fallen asleep while she was holding him on the couch, and this was her third attempt at putting him down. The other two times, he'd woken up.

This time, she'd left off the hall light and made sure to put on his sound machine before letting him go.

Slowly, she pulled her hands out from underneath him and held her breath. After five seconds of him not crying or even moving, she sighed with relief and silently pumped her fist in the air.

She truthfully didn't mind holding her sleeping nephew, but Piper and Nate were going to be home soon. She didn't want to leave them with a crying baby after their first night out alone together.

After waiting a few minutes just to make sure the baby was fully asleep, she turned to tiptoe out of the room, but her foot got caught on something. She tried to put her other foot out to catch herself, but it was tangled up in something else.

She put her hands out, scrambling to catch anything as she went down, but all they met was air.

She felt her head hit what had to be the dresser, and then it was lights out.

♡

"Tiana, Tiana. Tiana."

Tiana groaned as a headache ten times worse than any hangover she'd ever had descended upon her.

"Tiana, don't move."

Her eyes were closed, but she recognized the voice as her brother's.

"Wha...what..." She couldn't quite get the words out. It was like she couldn't catch her breath.

"You must have fallen, hit your head, and passed out. Don't worry; an ambulance is on the way."

Tiana did an internal check of the rest of her body and realized she was lying on her stomach.

She opened her eyes. *Oh shit.*

She attempted to push herself up on her hands and roll over, but she was too weak.

"Don't move," Nate commanded. "The 911 operator said to keep you still in case you have a neck injury."

Screw my neck.

"I can't...stay on...my stomach." She tried to take a deep breath. "The baby."

"Shh...it's okay. Piper has Wyatt. He's fine. He was sleeping when we got home and found you."

She shook her head—or started to anyway—but that movement was too painful, so she stopped. "Not your baby. My baby."

"Your baby?"

"I'm...I'm pregnant."

"What? What the fuck, Tiana?"

She didn't really care that she was shocking her brother right now. She needed to get on her back. "I'll...explain later. Please help."

Nate had just put his hands on her shoulders when Piper called out, "Nate, the paramedics are here."

"I think you should wait for them to come in the room."

Tiana wanted to cry. She hadn't felt the baby move once since she regained consciousness. She was trying not to panic, but she was really, really scared.

The sound of footsteps coming down the hall and at least

two people rushing into the room helped calm her somewhat. If she could get on her back and to the hospital, then everything would be okay.

It had to be.

The paramedics put a C collar around her neck and flipped her over onto their board.

"She's pregnant," Nate told them.

"We'll assess her in the ambulance and let the hospital know," the female paramedic said.

She met Tiana's eyes, and Tiana knew she could trust her.

They wheeled her down the hall and outside.

Nate turned around to look at Piper, who was standing in the doorway, holding Wyatt. "I'll meet you at the hospital," her brother said.

"Yes, of course, go. Don't forget to call your parents," Piper said. She looked at Tiana. "I'll come as soon as I can get someone to watch Wyatt."

"I'm sorry I ruined your night out," she said as they started loading her into the back.

She hadn't been loud enough for Piper to hear her, but Nate did.

"You don't worry about that. Worry about yourself." He glanced down at her belly. "And your baby." He looked up at her eyes again. "I'll call Dad and Trish."

"Can you make one more call?"

"Yes."

"Can you please call Ty and let him know? He's having dinner at his parents' tonight."

Nate raised his eyebrows in speculation. "Tiana, I'm sure

155

he's not going to concern himself too much about you coming home tonight. I know you've grown into friends, but this seems like a little much."

"You don't understand."

"Then, tell me."

"He's not just my roommate or my friend, Nate. He's the father."

"Sorry, this conversation will have to continue later," the female paramedic said and closed the door.

She sat across from Tiana and had a name on her uniform that read *Stevens*.

Tiana heard the front door of the ambulance open and close and the engine start.

Stevens shouted, "We're ready to go," to her partner in the front. Then, she looked at Tiana. "If your brother doesn't call your friend, I'll make sure the nurses know to do it." She smiled. "They're good about that."

"Thank you."

"You have enough to worry about without wondering if your..." Stevens trailed off as she pulled some stuff out of the compartments in the ambulance.

"Brother," Tiana supplied.

"Without wondering if your brother will call your friend."

"I'm kind of more worried that he will call him. Ty deserves a warning first."

"Your brother's going to be mad at your roommate for getting you pregnant?"

"No, my brother's going to be mad at his friend for getting me pregnant. I only recently became his roommate."

Stevens winced. "Ouch."

"You're telling me. If only I could warn him that Nate knows. Because there is no way my brother is okay with this."

CHAPTER TWENTY-EIGHT

After a long dinner, Naomi asked Ty, "Would you like to go and sit outside?"

"Yes, please," he said.

He saw his mom beaming out of the corner of his eye, but he ignored her. He didn't want to go outside to be alone. He wanted to get away from his mom trying to set him up.

The two of them went out the back and closed the door.

They sat down on the back steps, and Ty said, "I am so sorry about tonight. I don't know what my mother is thinking."

Naomi laughed. "Probably the same thing my mother is."

"As if we're not old enough to make our own decisions."

"I hear that," she said.

"I'm actually seeing someone. My mom doesn't know, but she suspects, and I think that's why she set up this dinner. What about you?"

"She thinks I'm married to my work, as if that were a

crime. I don't want to get married and have a bunch of babies."

"We should go in and tell them that we're going to Vegas to elope."

Naomi laughed. "I want to say yes, just to see the looks on their faces."

"And to know that their plan backfired in a big way. Would serve them right."

The two of them were laughing when he heard the back door open. Ty didn't bother turning around because he didn't feel like dealing with his mother right now, and it had to be her checking on them.

"You son of a bitch."

Ty whipped his head around. "Nate?" He jumped up. "What are you doing here?"

"I tried calling you several times, but it went straight to voice mail."

Ty yanked his phone from his pocket. "Damn it. It's dead." He hadn't noticed that it had died because he had put it on vibrate.

"Right."

Ty stepped closer to his friend. "What's wrong? Why are you pissed at me?"

"Because you fucking knocked up my sister!"

There was a gasp from the open door behind Nate.

"*Mon Dieu*," she muttered and looked to the sky.

Fuck.

It was his mother. This was not how he'd wanted to tell her.

Ty held up his hands. "I'm sorry, Nate. It wasn't on purpose. Tiana and I used protection, but it happened."

Nate's fists were opening and closing at his sides, and while Ty had no desire to get hurt, he really couldn't blame his friend if he punched him.

His mom crossed herself.

His father showed up. "Tyler, did I just hear that you got a woman pregnant?"

Everything was a mess, and this night might go down in history as the worst night ever.

"Yes, Dad. Please, take Mom inside. I will talk to the two of you later."

"That's my cue to go inside, too," Naomi said behind him.

Ty had forgotten she was there. Nate gave her the death glare as she went inside.

"You can stop," Ty said. "She and I were just talking."

"You two looked pretty fucking cozy to me."

"We were complaining about how our parents set us up without warning. That's it."

Nate crossed his arms over his chest. "I'm supposed to take the word of a liar?"

Ty pointed his finger at Nate. "I never actually lied to you. Tiana and I weren't ready to tell you yet."

Nate sneered. "Fine. I'm supposed to take the word of a predator?"

"Fuck you. Tiana is more than old enough."

"Yeah, well, I don't know many guys who convince girls to move into their house and then get them pregnant."

"First of all, she's a woman even if you don't want to

admit it. Second, she was pregnant *before* she moved in. That's why I offered her a place to stay, asshole."

"When the fuck did that happen?" Nate asked, his eyes blazing with anger.

Ty rubbed his forehead. "Your wedding."

"You fucker." Nate charged at him and punched him in the jaw.

Ty was momentarily pushed backward, and his eyes crossed. His vision returned just in time to see Nate take a swing at him again. Ty charged his friend and knocked him off his feet.

Ty stood while his friend scrambled to his feet. "I don't want to fight with you, Nate. I'm sorry, okay? It was an accident. Tiana and I didn't mean for it to happen, but we're both very excited."

Nate glared at him. "When you told me a while back that a girl you had a one-night stand with might be pregnant, you were talking about my sister, weren't you?"

Ty hung his head. "Yes."

"You are an asshole."

"I know, okay?" There was really nothing else to say. He'd slept with his friend's sister. He looked up. "Do you want to punch me again?"

"Yes. But it's hard when you don't hit back."

Ty shook his head. "I don't want to fight you."

"Does your face at least hurt?"

Ty cupped his jaw and moved it back and forth. "Like a fucking bitch."

Nate scoffed. "Good."

"That's cold, man."

Nate didn't say anything at first. "I know," he finally admitted.

"And you told my parents."

"At least I wasn't the only one you'd kept in the dark."

"Nate, we haven't told anyone, okay? You weren't the only one."

"That doesn't make me feel better. We were friends, dude."

Ty winced at Nate's use of the word *were*. He was going to let it go for now. Nate was upset.

But as Ty studied his friend, a thought occurred to him.

"Nate? How did you find out?" Tiana and Ty had agreed to tell Nate together. "I thought Tiana was babysitting for you tonight."

A guilty look crossed Nate's face. "She was. Piper and I got home and found Tiana unconscious on the floor. She must have fallen and hit her head. While we waited for the ambulance, she told me about the baby. She was worried."

Ty stomped forward and grabbed Nate's shirt in his fist. "You dick. She's in the hospital, and you're here, fighting with me?" Ty pushed Nate away and ran into the house, heading to the front door.

"Where are you going, Tyler?" his mom demanded.

"I need to get to the hospital."

"We need to talk."

"Mom, not right now, okay? Tiana is in the hospital, and she's pregnant. With your grandchild."

His mom gasped again and put a hand to her mouth. She might not be the most open to the idea of Tiana being pregnant, but she would never wish harm on anyone, especially not her unborn grandchild.

Ty hurried over and kissed her on the side of the head. "We'll talk later, okay?"

She nodded.

Ty looked at his dad and got the same nod.

He turned to his parents' guests. "Sorry for ruining dinner, but I have to go."

"By all means," Ben said.

Ty turned to Nate. "Now, tell me what hospital she's at."

CHAPTER TWENTY-NINE

Tiana opened her eyes and saw Ty sleeping in the chair beside her.

"Ty," she said in a low voice. It was painful to talk.

Even though the doctors had given her pain medication, her head still hurt. She reached up to find the spot where she'd hit her head.

"Don't touch it," Ty said.

She dropped her hand and smiled at him. "Does it look awful?"

He smiled and shook his head. "No. It's covered with a bandage, but it'll hurt more if you touch it."

"How do you know?"

"I played sports in high school. Trust me, I've been where you are a few times."

She snorted. "I doubt you tripped over something and hit your head on a dresser."

"Okay, so mine were all sports-related, but I still know what an injury feels like."

She smiled at him. "Thanks for coming."

"Tiana, if you feel the need to thank me, then we need to have a talk about our relationship."

She laughed. "Did they tell you about the baby?"

Ty slowly shook his head. "Your brother said you fell on your belly, but after that, he didn't know what had happened. Your parents left when I got here, and the doctors and nurses won't tell me anything because of privacy."

He looked like he wanted to ask but didn't want to at the same time.

Tiana started crying without warning.

Ty grabbed her hand, and his eyes filled with tears, too. "Oh, Tiana, I'm so sorry."

She shook her head and tried to talk. "No-no—" She couldn't get the words out because she was crying too hard.

"Shh...you don't have to say it."

She pulled her hand out from under his and cupped his cheek. "I'm sorry—"

"You don't have to be sorry."

Tiana laughed through her tears. "Will you let me finish?"

Startled by her change in demeanor, Ty clamped his mouth shut.

"I was going to say, I'm sorry for scaring you."

Ty frowned in confusion.

"Everything is fine with the baby. It's just my head that they're worried about."

Ty picked up her hand again and brought it to his forehead. "Oh, thank God." He looked down at her bed. "Thank you, thank you, thank you." He sighed with relief and looked up at her. A tear fell from his eye and landed on his cheek. "You really scared me."

"I'm sorry." She pulled her hand from his grip and wiped away his tear. "I was just so happy when they told me everything was okay that I started crying. And I guess the memory is still fresh, and I started crying again."

Ty reached forward and wiped the tears from her face. "Shh...don't be sorry. I should have let you finish."

Tiana laughed. "Wow. A man apologizing for interrupting."

"I think the doctor needs to come in here again and look at you. Check that head injury. You're making sexist jokes about us men."

"Oh, Ty," she said and dropped her head back against the bed. "I was so scared."

"I know, honey."

She opened her eyes. "Were my parents nice to you?"

He seemed to think about it. "Not super nice, but not mean either. I think they were just worried about you, ya know."

She nodded. "I really messed up how I went about telling my family. But at least we still have yours."

Ty chuckled. "Uh, no, we don't. Your brother came to my parents' house, where I was having dinner, and pretty much yelled at me in front of everyone. My parents definitely know now."

Tiana groaned. "Oh my God, I'm sorry. I told him to call you. Not go to your parents' house and find you."

Ty shrugged. "My phone had died. He didn't really have a choice. And, Tiana?"

She met his eyes.

"If it came down to me not knowing until I was alone or finding out right away and having my parents know, I'd pick the latter."

She smiled. "That's sweet." She took a closer look at him and squinted. "Is it my imagination, or is your nose swollen?"

Ty touched his face and winced. "You're not imagining anything. Your brother punched me."

She gasped and cupped her mouth. "He didn't."

"I'm sorry. Maybe I shouldn't have told you."

She shook her head a little too hard because the pain exploded. "Ow!"

Ty stood up. "Are you okay? Do you need a doctor?"

"No. I just moved too fast." She grabbed his hand. "I don't want you to keep something like Nate starting a fight with you from me, okay?"

Ty nodded and sat back down. "Maybe you should go back to sleep."

She yawned again. He was probably right. "I thought you weren't supposed to sleep if you had a head injury or concussion."

"That's not true anymore. You need sleep to heal. So, you should do that. And I'll be here when you wake up."

"Thank you."

"Do you need anything while you rest? I can run home and pick up some stuff."

She only needed him. "Will you lie with me?"

His eyebrows shot up his forehead. "I don't think that's allowed."

"I don't care. What are they going to do, kick me out?"

Ty chuckled. "Good point. All right, move over."

Tiana moved to the side and handed him the remote as he lay down. "Here. Watch what you want."

He kissed her on the forehead. "Will do. Now, sleep."

Tiana woke sometime later, feeling a little better. Her head still hurt but not as much. The fluttering in her belly helped ease the pain.

Her eyes adjusted to the dim light in her room, and she looked to the doorway to see her brother standing there.

"Are you going to come in?" she asked in a low voice because Ty was sleeping beside her.

Nate put his hands in his pockets and entered her room. His eyes landed on his friend in her bed, and he frowned even more than he already had been.

"I know you're disappointed, but there's nothing you can do to change the situation," she said.

Nate scowled. "I'm not disappointed. I'm pissed off, Tiana."

"Nate..." she started but stopped when Ty stirred.

He opened his eyes and smiled at her until he noticed Nate was in the room. His smile fell as quickly as it had appeared.

Ty huffed out a deep breath and sat up. "I'll let you two talk."

"You don't have to leave," Tiana told him.

"Yeah, I do." He kissed her on the temple. "At least for a little bit. I'll be back soon, and I'll stay in the hospital. Call me if you need me." He slid out of her bed and went out the door.

She looked at her brother. "Are you happy? He left."

Nate scoffed and plopped down on the chair next to her bed. "No, I'm not happy. I don't want this for you."

"Don't want what?"

"For you to be pregnant. Like this."

She raised her brow.

"Without a husband. I mean, what are you and Ty anyway?"

Her brother had a little bit of a point. But just a little.

"I don't know, Nate. It's complicated, okay?"

"Are you dating? Is he your boyfriend? Are you just friends? Roommates?"

She sighed. "I just said, it's complicated. If you really want to know the dirty deets, we slept together at your wedding, and I got pregnant. I didn't see him for three months until I showed up on his doorstep to tell him. He was super supportive from the very beginning. When he found out I needed a place to stay, he offered me his spare room. But to be honest, I've never slept a day in my bed. I've spent every night with Ty, and yes, we're having sex."

Nate winced.

"Hey, you asked."

"But you don't know if you're dating?" he asked in disbelief.

"I suppose we are, but we've never talked about it. We've never made it official."

"Don't you think you should? You're having a baby together."

"I don't know, Nate. With the pregnancy and figuring out when we were going to tell everyone, it's been nice to just see where Ty and I were going without pressure."

Nate didn't look like he appreciated her answer.

"Can I just remind you that, about a year ago, you slept with your dead friend's wife and got her pregnant?"

Nate looked horrified. "Ouch, Ti. That was a low blow."

"I'm just trying to show you that things aren't always black and white or as simple as they sound. Obviously, there's more to you and Piper, but someone could take that explanation and condemn you for it."

Nate smiled and held up his hands. "Okay, I surrender. You have a very valid point."

She stuck her nose up in the air. "I know I do."

"How'd you get so smart?"

"Because I'm not a child anymore, Nate. I know it's hard for you to see that. But I'm a grown woman who knows what she wants. And I want this baby. And I want Ty."

Nate nodded. "I understand."

"I am sorry you had to find out this way though. Ty and I had planned on telling you together."

"I'm sorry you had an accident at my house."

"Do you know what I tripped on?"

Nate looked away, ashamed. "My shoes."

Tiana fake gasped. "Your shoes? Bro, you owe me so hard."

He met her eyes again. "I know. Piper's always yelling at me that I take them off and just leave them in the middle of the floor. She's never going to let me live this down."

"Ha. Serves you right."

Footsteps sounded at the door, and both of them looked up to see Ty had returned with a cup of coffee.

"I think you should go talk to him," Tiana told her brother in a low voice.

"Yeah, you're probably right."

CHAPTER THIRTY

Nate walked out of Tiana's room but stopped Ty before he could enter. "Can we talk?"

Ty was a little shocked that they were going to have this conversation this soon, but he wasn't going to complain.

"Of course." Ty looked around. "Do you want to go and walk outside?"

"That sounds good."

Ty looked at Tiana from the doorway. "We'll be back."

She nodded. "I'll be here."

Ty smiled and closed her door, so she could rest. "Let's go," he said to Nate.

The two of them walked in silence as they made their way to the front doors. Ty didn't want to say anything until they were out of earshot of people in case Nate yelled or threw a punch at him again.

When they got outside, Ty waited for Nate to speak.

"What did you want to say?" Ty asked after Nate had been silent for too long.

"My sister likes you."

That was not what Ty had expected to hear. "That's good because I like her, too."

"Does she know that?"

"Yes."

Nate stopped walking and turned to Ty. "But does she really? Because when I asked her what was going on between you two, she said it was complicated."

Ty shrugged. "She's not wrong."

Nate frowned.

"Look, I like your sister. A lot. But I think the whole pregnancy thing has made things unconventional. I didn't really plan on seeing Tiana again, but then she showed up, pregnant. But I'm so happy she did. I like having her in my life. I like living with her. And I can't help but be excited for the baby."

"But..." Nate prompted.

"There's really no *but*. I actually realized last night at my parents' that I had not been forthcoming enough with Tiana in how I felt about her."

"Are you sure there's no *but*?"

Ty smiled. "Okay, you're right. There is a *but*."

Nate narrowed his eyes. "I knew it."

"*But*...I'm worried she'll only think I like her because of the baby. I want her to know that I like her with or without a baby. I'm worried she won't believe me."

Nate relaxed. "That actually wasn't a bad *but*."

Ty smiled. "That's why I initially said there wasn't one."

His smile fell. "You know, if she wasn't your sister, I would have so many things to ask you in hopes that you could offer advice."

Nate looked a little guilty. "How about I forget for a moment that she is my sister? I'll try and think back to that day at work when you told me you might be a father."

"If you're trying to make me feel guilty, you've succeeded. And I thought you were going to forget for a moment?" Ty asked.

"Okay, okay. You're right." Nate took a deep breath. "Hit me."

To make the conversation as painless as possible, Ty decided not to use Tiana's name. "There's this woman I slept with months ago, and she's pregnant."

Nate nodded.

"We just found out we're having a girl."

Nate's head flung up. "Really?"

Ty smiled. "Really."

"I'm going to have a niece," Nate said with his first genuine smile. He shook his head as if to clear his thoughts. "Sorry. Continue."

"I didn't really expect anything to happen after our night together, but to tell you the truth, I wouldn't have minded giving it a shot. Unfortunately, I woke up the next day alone."

Nate made a choking sound.

Ty gave him a look.

"Sorry. Keep going."

The two of them started walking, and Ty kept his eyes in front of him. "Because the woman didn't stick around, I didn't contact her. I thought she'd made it clear how she felt about me. So, when she showed up pregnant, I'm not going to lie and say I wasn't stressed out at first. But after the initial panic, I was excited. And the more time I spent with this woman, the more I liked her. I even invited her to live with me—no strings attached—so she'd have a place to stay, and we could take care of the baby together. But things have progressed with us, and now, I'm falling in love with her."

"Ty, you need to tell her."

"But what if she doesn't feel that way about me? She didn't want to date me before. What if she's only dating me now because she feels she has no choice?" He looked at his friend. "I will do whatever she needs for the baby. Whatever. And I will do whatever she wants as far as us being a couple. But I will not be some consolation prize."

"I know it's going to be hard, but you need to talk to her. You need to tell her how you feel and what you're worried about. Take it from me that a lot can be misunderstood when you just assume what the other person thinks."

"You and Piper?"

Nate nodded. "Oh, yeah. I almost messed it up between us." He stopped and turned to Ty. "And listen, I know this woman you're talking about. She's got a beautiful heart, but she wouldn't string someone along. Did she ever tell you about her ex-boyfriend, Anthony?"

Ty shook his head. "No."

"Anthony was older." Nate smirked. "She has a thing for old men."

"Hey, we're basically the same age."

Nate laughed. "Okay, okay. She likes older men. And

Anthony made some good money. He offered to let her live with him for free."

That sounded familiar.

"And he was going to pay for her master's degree."

"What?" Ty was shocked.

Nate nodded. "Swear to God."

"What happened?"

Nate shrugged. "She didn't like him that much, and she wasn't going to stick around and be with someone just for money."

"Wow," Ty said, amazed that he hadn't known this about Tiana.

"Yeah. Of course, now, I'm thinking she should have stayed with Anthony because there is no way she's going to school in the fall." Nate's tone was teasing, but Ty knew his friend was partly serious.

"Just so you know, Tiana and I have that figured out. You're right. She's not going to school in the fall, but depending on how she feels, she'll go in the spring or next fall. I'm not going to let her get away with not going. I know how much it means to her."

"I appreciate that."

"That's nice and all, but I'm not doing it for you. I'm doing it for her."

Nate nodded in understanding as they headed back for the hospital.

CHAPTER THIRTY-ONE

Two days later, Tiana's mom walked with her as the nurse pushed her in a wheelchair toward the front door.

"There's your father," her mom said, pointing out the big glass window.

Tiana looked behind her at the nurse. "Thanks. I've got it from here." She slowly stood so as to not jolt her head with any sudden movements, and she walked outside.

She closed her eyes and inhaled deeply.

"Are you okay?" her mom asked.

"Yes, Mom. I'm simply enjoying the fresh air after being in a hospital room the last two days."

"Sorry, honey. I'm just worried about you."

Tiana opened her eyes. "I know. But I'll be fine. I'm not the first person to hit their head, and I won't be the last. Nate had at least one concussion in high school from sports."

"Yes, but..."

"But what, Mom?"

"He wasn't pregnant."

Tiana rolled her eyes. "Mom, the baby is in my uterus, not my head. The baby is fine. The OB said so."

Her father honked the horn and stuck his head out the window. "What are you waiting for?" he yelled.

Tiana laughed. "We'd better go."

"He has the patience of a saint," her mother said sarcastically as they walked to the car.

Her mom helped her in, even after she protested, and then got in the backseat with her.

"Are you sure you don't want to come home with us?" her mom asked her for the hundredth time as they took off.

"No, Mom. I appreciate it, but I want to go home."

"Is Ty's house really home?"

Her parents and she hadn't really talked about her getting pregnant out of wedlock yet. Tiana was pretty sure that once she was better, that conversation would come. And she had to wonder if that was part of why her mom was concerned about her not coming to their house.

But Tiana didn't even have to think about the answer. "Yes, it is."

"I'm just afraid he won't know how to take care of you," her mom said, concern in her eyes.

"Mom, I really don't need anyone to take care of me. The doctor even said I could go to work in two days."

Her mom pursed her lips. "I don't think that's a good idea."

"If I'm not feeling up to it, I'll stay home."

"Good."

Tiana closed her eyes and started dozing off when her

mom woke her up.

"I'm just saying, Tiana, if Ty could take care of you, then why isn't he here?"

"Because you refused to take no for an answer when you told Tiana you were taking her home," her dad said from up front.

"Thanks, Dad."

Her mother sniffled and stuck her nose in the air. "She's my baby. I refuse to apologize."

Now that Tiana was going to have her own baby, she was starting to understand how much her mom loved her. Tiana reached over and grabbed her mom's hand. Her mom looked at her.

"I love you, Mom."

Her mom's eyes filled with tears. "I love you, too." She reached over and touched Tiana's stomach with her free palm. "And I already love this baby."

Tiana squeezed her mom's hand. "I'm glad. You're going to be a great grandma."

"Going to be? I already am."

Tiana laughed. "Sorry. Of course. I forgot how much you spoil Wyatt."

"I don't spoil him."

Tiana snorted. "He has every toy ever made, and he can't even crawl yet."

Her mom shrugged. "Then, they'll be there when he can."

"Will you spoil my baby as much? Even though my circumstances are different from Nate's?"

Her mom squeezed her hand this time. "Absolutely."

CHAPTER THIRTY-TWO

Ty heard a vehicle pull up in his driveway, and he ran out to help Tiana out of the car. It had almost killed him to not be the one to bring her home, but she had explained how it was important for her parents to be the ones to do it.

He was just glad they weren't taking her to their house. He wanted her with him, and he'd missed her the last few days.

"Hey," he said as he offered her his hand.

She grinned at him. "Hey."

He hadn't told her yet how he felt about her because he wanted to wait until she was home, but seeing her beautiful smile almost made him blurt out that he loved her.

"Do you mind if I help you up to the house?" he asked her.

"I'd love that," she said, taking his arm.

Her dad grabbed her bag and handed it to Ty. "Here you go. You'd best take care of that now."

Ty nodded because he understood Jerome wasn't talking about the luggage; he was talking about his daughter.

As the two of them walked toward the front door, he heard Trish say, "I thought we were going inside."

Jerome said something, but Ty couldn't hear the words.

"Did you want your parents to come in?"

"Don't tell them I said this, but no. I just want to lie down and rest for a bit. Maybe watch some reality TV and enjoy being home."

"I like the sound of that."

"Sitting on the couch and watching TV?"

"No. The *you being home* part."

They reached the front door. Ty set the bag down, so he could open the door for her before picking it back up and following her in.

"How did everything go here? Did I miss anything while I was gone?" Tiana asked him as she sat on the couch.

Ty shook his head. "I was at the hospital or work, so you didn't miss anything." That was mostly the truth. He did have a small surprise for Tiana that he'd been working on the last few days. "But I took today and tomorrow off, so I could be home with you."

Tiana frowned. "You didn't have to do that."

"I want to do that."

She smiled and looked away. "Thank you."

"Are you hungry? I can make you something to eat."

"Yes, please. But nothing too fancy. You should enjoy your day off."

"How about soup?"

"Soup sounds good."

"I'll be back."

Ty went into the kitchen and opened his lazy Susan. He hadn't realized all the different types of soup he had in there until he started pulling them out. He didn't even remember buying half of them because he wasn't a big soup person.

"Hey, Tiana?" he said as he walked back into the living room.

He was about to ask her which one she wanted to eat, but he saw that she was lying down and asleep. He quietly tiptoed up to the couch, pulled off the blanket that hung on the back, and gently spread it over her.

Tiana woke to sunlight streaming on her face and soaked in the warmth before opening her eyes. It was so nice to be home.

She opened her lids and looked around. The house was quiet, and no one was in the room.

"Ty?" She cleared her throat and said his name again a little louder, "Ty?"

She heard footsteps coming from upstairs.

"Hey, you're awake."

She sat up. "Sorry, I didn't mean to crash."

"No need to apologize. You needed your sleep. Are you hungry? I can go make you something now that you're awake."

"Yes, please. But let me help."

Ty pointed a finger at her. "Don't you dare. Your job is to find some reality TV and binge-watch it."

"Yes, sir," she mocked jokingly.

Ty laughed and walked to the kitchen.

Tiana grabbed the remote from the end table and went searching for something fun to watch.

Ty came in to ask her what kind of soup she wanted, and after she answered, he disappeared again.

An hour later, Tiana was feeling good. She'd gotten some rest, some relaxation, and some food in her stomach. She was starting to feel better, and she bet that by the next morning, she'd feel even closer to her normal self.

She insisted on carrying her own bowl to the sink when Ty tried to take it from her. "I don't want you waiting on me hand and foot."

Ty shrugged. "I can't help it. I'm worried."

"How about I won't hide when I need help and you don't keep doing everything for me?"

He smiled. "Okay, fine." He looked toward the stairs. "Can I show you something?"

"If it's your penis, I've already seen it."

Ty's expression turned horrified. "I wouldn't ask you to have sex now."

Tiana burst out laughing. "Oh, man, that was a *joke*. But if I had known you were going to react like that, I would have recorded you."

He shook his head. "Not funny."

"I disagree. Now, show me what's upstairs."

They walked upstairs and went past her room and the

spare bathroom, but they didn't go into the master bedroom. Instead, they approached the closed door of the third bedroom.

"Can you close your eyes?"

Tiana closed them. "Okay, I'm ready."

She heard the doorknob turn and the door swing open.

"You can open them."

Tiana slowly opened her eyes, not sure what to expect.

Inside the room was a fully prepared nursery. There was a crib along the wall and a matching dresser on the opposite side. There was a changing table that was stocked with everything under the sun. In the corner was a rocking chair, and all the decorations were the ones they had picked out together.

"I hope this is okay. I know we talked about doing it together, but I wanted to surprise you when you got home," Ty said from behind her.

She only nodded because she was afraid her voice would be too shaky if she tried to speak.

"Are you okay?" he asked.

She swung around and threw herself in his arms. "It's perfect."

She could almost feel the relief pour off of him as he pulled her into a hug. "I'm so glad you approve."

She let Ty hold her for a minute or two before she pulled away. "What did you do all this for?"

He looked away, embarrassed. "Because I wanted to show you that I love you. I didn't feel that just saying it was enough." He met her eyes. "I know we pretty much got together because of the baby, but I love being with you. I'm so happy that you're the mother of my child." He swallowed.

"When I thought you'd lost the baby, my first reaction after being devastated was that I wanted to make things better for you and that I wanted to try again as soon as you were ready." He kissed her forehead. "I want you to know that I want you with or without this baby."

Tiana buried her face in his chest and started crying. To his credit, Ty didn't demand to know what was wrong; he just held her again.

When she felt like she could compose herself, she looked up at him. "I love you, too. And while this baby has shaken some things up in my life, it's the best thing that's ever happened to me because it brought me to you."

Ty pumped a fist in the air and hooted.

Tiana laughed at him. She was so happy that he was happy.

"Can you do me one favor before this baby is born then?" he asked her.

"Anything," she said.

"I want you to marry me."

She arched up and kissed him on the mouth. "You got it."

CHAPTER THIRTY-THREE

Ty walked Tiana up to his parents' house, and he could see how nervous she was.

He took her hand in his. "It's going to be okay. I promise."

"Your mom doesn't like me."

"She doesn't know you. That's why we're doing this." His mom had confessed to him that she thought Tiana was too young for him. She had been worried that Tiana liked him because he had a job and was stable.

But he was convinced that once his mom gave Tiana a chance, she'd realize Tiana was mature and was with Ty for the right reasons.

"So you say."

He pulled his hand from hers and put his arm around her. "No matter what, I'm on your side. If my mother doesn't like it, that's too bad for her."

She looked up at his face. "Thank you."

He kissed her. "No thanks needed. That's what partners are supposed to do."

When they reached the front door, Ty knocked before opening it. "Mom? Dad? We're here."

Ty's dad came into view first. "Evening, you two. How are you?"

"Nervous," Tiana blurted out.

Ty's dad laughed and leaned in. "Don't be. Her bark is worse than her bite. Plus, she's making coq au vin, one of her specialties. She doesn't make that for everyone."

Tiana looked at Ty, and he nodded.

"Dad's right. This is a good sign."

They followed his dad into the kitchen to find his mom cooking away.

"Ty and Tiana are here," his dad announced and headed off to the living room.

She looked up and smiled at them. "*Bonjour.*"

"Hi, *Maman.*"

His mom beamed.

When he was little, he'd called her *Maman*, but as he'd gotten older and all his friends had started calling their mothers *Mom*, he'd stopped using the French version. He supposed it had made her sad, but she'd never said anything.

Now that he was older and didn't have to worry about fitting in with his friends, he called her that sometimes to make her happy. She always loved it when he did.

"*Maman?*" Tiana said. "That's so pretty."

His mother's eyes widened, and she winced.

"Oh no. What did I do wrong?" Tiana asked him.

Ty laughed and shook his head. "Your accent is atrocious."

His mom reached over and patted Tiana on the hand. "Don't you worry, *chère*. We'll fix that right up."

"Thank you." She turned to Ty. "This is why you need to teach the baby French right away. That way, she won't have a bad American accent."

Ty noticed his mom looked like she was about to cry. "Truthfully, I'm not fluent. I don't quite know all the words. Every once in a while, I have to insert an English word in there if I'm speaking French to my mom."

Tiana narrowed her eyes at him. "But I know for a fact that Piper said that you said something to her in French the first time you met her."

Ty laughed. "You heard about that, huh?" He shrugged. "Like I said, I don't know all the words. My mom would be much better at teaching the baby."

His mom spoke up, "It is true. My Tyler moved here when he was four. There were many times he didn't want to speak French anymore."

"Mom, that's not exactly right. I only wanted to learn English like all the kids at school."

"Will you teach our baby French, Mrs. Morgan?" Tiana asked hesitantly.

"Of course, *chère*. And you can call me Cleo."

Tiana beamed. "Thank you, Cleo."

"Now, how much do you know about cooking?" his mom asked.

Later, Ty would have to tell Tiana that this was his mom's

way of apologizing. She didn't let just anyone help her in the kitchen.

"I know how to cook, but I've never made this dish before."

"Would you like to learn? I already taught Tyler, but he always messes it up."

Ty threw his hands up in the air. "Mom, I make it just fine. I'm just not as good of a cook as you."

"That is a fact," his mom said with a straight face.

"Gee, thanks."

His mother ignored him. "Come in, Tiana, and grab a knife. You can help me with the vegetables."

"You'll be okay in here?" Ty asked Tiana.

She nodded.

"I'll just be in the other room if you need me."

"Okay."

Ty went to find his father. "Dad, what happened with Mom?"

His father sat up in his seat. "What do you mean?"

"She's being so nice to Tiana. She's done a one-eighty since the last time they were together."

His father smiled. "Let's just say, the two of us had a nice talk. I told her that if she wanted to exclude Tiana from the family, there was a strong chance she was going to exclude her grandchild as well. Especially now that the two of you are getting married."

Ty sat down. "I would never keep the baby from Mom."

He smiled and looked sympathetically at him. "I know that, son. But it wouldn't be good for the child to have animosity between his mother and grandmother."

His father was right.

"It's a girl," he corrected his father.

His dad's eyes widened. "It is?"

Ty nodded.

"That's excellent news. It will be nice to have a little girl running around here. Your mom is going to be so excited."

"I'm pretty excited, too, Dad."

His father smiled. "Me, too, son."

EPILOGUE

Several Years Later

Tiana pulled into the garage after a long day at work. She had stayed late again and was glad to be home. She loved her job as a forensic accountant, and she often got lost in all the numbers, but she loved her family more. And there was nothing better than coming home to them.

Ty had kept his promise to help her go to grad school. To help save money, they had decided to elope instead of having a wedding before she had the baby. She had ended up waiting a year to get her master's. With their daughter so little, she hadn't wanted to worry about studying and taking care of a baby. Tiana had quit her job, so she could go to school full-time and finish in a year. Something she wouldn't have been able to do on her own, even without a baby.

Sometimes, things worked out better than people thought they would.

When she walked in the door, all she heard was screaming from young voices. She knew the kids were playing.

She made sure to shut the door loudly and then shouted, "Mommy's home."

The screaming stopped for a few seconds and then started again and got closer until two little whirlwinds ran into her legs.

"Mommy, Mommy, Mommy," they chanted.

"Yes, children?"

"You're home," five-year-old Jada said.

Just like children to state the obvious.

"Yes, I am, sweetie."

Tiana reached down and picked up two-and-a-half-year-old Malik.

"Mommy," he said.

She kissed his cheek. "Hey, baby."

"Where's Daddy?" Tiana asked Jada.

"In the living room, picking up toys."

Tiana lifted her eyebrows. "Don't you think you should be picking up toys?"

Jada put a finger by her mouth. "Hmm." She dropped her hand. "No."

"No? And why not?"

"Because Daddy is better at doing it."

"Kid, someday, you're going to run the world with that logic." Tiana stepped around her daughter. "Let's go help Daddy clean up."

"I don't want to run the world," Jada said from behind her mother.

"What do you want to do?"

"Hmm," she said again. "I want to be a singer."

Tiana didn't have the heart to tell her little girl that she couldn't carry a tune in the slightest. Besides, she was five; her voice might change.

"I was hoping you'd want to do what Mommy does."

"Boring. I've been to your work, and it's boring."

"What's boring?" Ty asked when they entered the room.

Tiana set Malik down on the floor, and he ran to his toys. "My job, apparently."

Ty chuckled and then cried out when Malik pulled out at least ten toys in two seconds, "I just picked all those up."

"Are you still glad I showed up on your doorstep?"

Ty scowled. "Don't ask me that right now. I also cleaned a horrible diaper right before you got home and wiped glitter from all over the table."

Tiana covered her mouth and tried not to laugh, but it was too hard.

"It's not funny."

"It kind of is, babe." She took a step forward and kissed him on the cheek. "You're a good daddy though." She looked down at Jada. "Daddy's a good daddy, right?"

Jada clapped her hands. "He's the best daddy in the whole world," she said as she spread her hands wide.

"See," Tiana said, and the corners of Ty's mouth lifted.

Ty picked up Jada. "Okay, I guess we'll keep you," he said and gave her a bear hug.

Jada giggled. "Daddy, your beard is scratching me."

"Sorry, baby," he said and pulled back to look at her face. "What do you want for dinner?"

"Ice cream."

"We're not having ice cream for dinner," Tiana said. "Pick again."

Jada put her hands on Ty's face and squeezed his cheeks together. "Ice cream," she said again. "See, Mommy, Daddy wants ice cream, too."

"How about ice cream for dessert?" Ty asked.

"Okay."

"Malik, what do you want for dinner?" Tiana asked even though she already knew what the answer would be. It was the same every time.

"Fries," her son said as he pulled out more toys.

"Fries and chicken nuggets or fries and a burger?" Tiana asked.

"Fries."

"But what do you want with the fries?"

"Fries."

Tiana threw her hands up. "It's Friday. Should we just go get fast food? We can have fries and ice cream, and then everyone will be happy, including us because then we won't have to cook."

Ty leaned over and kissed Tiana. "That sounds like a really good idea." He put Jada down. "Go put on your shoes, kiddo."

Malik heard the word *shoes* and raced after his sister. "Me, too, shoes. Me, too, shoes."

After the two of them darted around the corner, Ty pulled Tiana into his arms. "How was work today?"

She laid her hand on his strong chest. "Good. I finished

up my latest project before I walked out the door, so I don't have to worry about it this weekend. What about you? Did you have a good day?"

"Yes. Nothing great happened, but nothing bad either. I like those kinds of days."

"I know you do."

"Oh, but your brother did stop by my cubicle. He wants us to come to dinner tomorrow night with your parents."

"No cooking two nights in a row? Count me in."

Ty laughed. "And this way, our kids can mess up someone else's house."

Tiana chuckled. "Someday, they'll clean up after themselves."

Ty snorted. "Yeah, after they move out."

The sound of Jada running back into the room pulled them apart.

"Mommy, Malik can't get his shoes on."

The slap of something hitting the floor over and over could be heard, and Malik entered the room, wearing one of Ty's shoes. "I ready," he said.

Tiana and Ty laughed as Ty picked up their son and tickled him. "That's my shoe, you little thief."

Malik laughed.

"Let's go find your actual shoes," Ty said and walked out of the room with Malik.

"Mommy, I put on my shoes."

Tiana looked down. "Good job, sweetie."

Jada beamed from the praise and ran after her father and brother.

Tiana followed behind them with a smile on her face. She had the best life, and it was no longer complicated. Some would even call it mundane.

But Tiana loved it.

FRIENDS WITH BENEFITS SAMPLE
CHAPTER ONE

Elise Phillips scanned the bar and grill as the door closed, leaving the June warmth behind her.

An arm toward the back of the room shot up, waving. Next, she saw her college friend's light-brown hair, and then Rachel Garwood's pixie face lit up as she beckoned her to the table.

When Elise approached, Rachel stood and squealed, her hazel eyes shining, as she held out her arms for a hug. Rachel had to step on her tippy-toes while Elise had to bend down. Elise was five-seven, but Rachel was only five-two.

"I'm so happy you're here," Rachel said. "I can't believe you get to come out with us whenever you want now."

About a month ago, Elise had moved back to the Minneapolis-St. Paul area, where she'd gone to high school and college. She'd found out her father was sick, and she wanted to be close to him just in case he didn't have much time left. Even though Rachel had also been born and raised in the Twin Cities, they hadn't met until they became room-mates at the University of Minnesota.

"Me either," she said as she stepped back from her friend.

"So, how's the house-hunt going?" Rachel asked as she took her seat.

Elise sighed as she hung her purse on the edge of the chair next to Rachel and sat next to her. "Okay. I'm so glad my old house sold; that's a relief. I really like the realtor you referred, but so far, I haven't found something I really like and want to buy."

"I'm so glad you like Cara. She's great. And I know what you mean. Sean probably would have been happy with the ten other houses we saw, but I didn't have that I-could-live-here feeling." Rachel had just bought a home with her fiancé, Sean, about six months earlier. "I'm sure you'll find one you like sooner rather than later."

"I hope so. I can only live with my parents for so long before they drive me completely nuts. I'm twenty-nine, but sometimes, I think they forget that I've been living on my own for over a decade."

"Ah, they're sweet."

Elise snorted. "You don't have to live with them."

Her mother had always been protective, but her hovering had gotten worse ever since her father was diagnosed with colon cancer.

"Well, let's agree to disagree. I'm just happy you're home."

So was she. Elise had enjoyed living in Denver since finishing graduate school, but it felt good to be home. And, while she would miss it, she didn't regret coming back once she learned her father was sick.

Elise gestured to the four open seats at the table. "Who else is coming?"

"Do you remember Shelly and Joe Howard?"

"Hmm." Elise couldn't quite remember them off the top of her head. "Oh. Did I meet them one year at your Christmas party? Shelly teaches with you, and her boyfriend is Joe. Both redheads?"

"Yes, that's them. Although they're husband and wife now. Shelly is actually pregnant. They are going to have the cutest little ginger baby."

Elise chuckled. "That's so great for them," she said, meaning it even though she felt slightly let down.

When Rachel had asked her to have dinner and drinks, Elise had assumed it was going to be a girls' thing. While she remembered liking Shelly and Joe, they were a couple, which meant one of the six seats belonged to Sean. So, either it was a couples' get-together and Rachel was setting her up with someone or she was going to be the dreaded fifth wheel. Neither option sounded appealing.

"So, Shelly, Joe, and Sean are coming. Is the sixth seat someone you're trying to hook me up with?" she asked just as Rachel said, "Oh, look. There are Shelly and Joe now."

Her friend stood and waved to catch the newcomers' attention.

Despite the two of them speaking at the same time, Rachel had heard her question. She sat back down and cocked her head. "I wouldn't do that to you. I know how much you hate being set up on blind dates."

Fifth wheel, it was then. Elise didn't know whether to be relieved that she wouldn't have to fake interest in someone—because she really didn't have the energy for that tonight—or disappointed that she was going to be the poor single girl.

Turned out neither because Rachel then said, "No, the last seat is for Luke Long. Do you remember him?"

Elise's answer was a groan of irritation. Oh, she remembered him all right. So did every other member of the student body—at least, those with ovaries. Girls' IQs dropped when Luke was around. It almost made her embarrassed to be a member of the female sex.

Thankfully, Shelly and Joe walked up, so Rachel didn't hear her response because Elise knew Sean and Luke had been good friends in college. Greetings were made, and Elise was reintroduced to the couple considering it had been a few years since she last saw them. They talked about Shelly's ever-expanding belly. She was huge, but she still had seven weeks to go. Shelly was barely over five feet while Joe was a former football player and closer to six feet tall, and they joked about how she was going to have an enormous baby. Thankfully, the group's joking had Elise almost forgetting all about the previous conversation.

When the door opened, she was sure she could feel a breeze all the way at the back of the room as Sean and Luke walked in. The two of them contrasted each other. Sean was blond and blue-eyed and only about five-eight while Luke was over six feet with thick dark brown hair and chocolate-brown eyes. Sean was showing Luke something on his phone, and Luke threw his head back and laughed, catching all the attention in the room. Elise swore she saw drool on a couple of ladies' chins.

Barf.

To be fair, Luke wasn't a horrible person, and she hadn't seen him in years, since college, so he'd probably matured... hopefully. But, back in school, he'd been quite the man-slut. While he hadn't been truly arrogant—she'd known some conceited assholes, and Luke had never been like that—he was gorgeous, and he knew it. Girls had practically thrown themselves at him, and he'd had no shame, sleeping his way through the female student body and leaving a trail of broken hearts.

Elise hadn't been a saint. She'd had a few one-night stands and even a couple of exclusive friends with benefits, but she'd like to think she'd had some discretion. She certainly hadn't slept with every guy who had hit on her.

Luke looked at one of the girls—probably ten years his junior—who was staring wide-eyed at him, and he winked at her.

Elise rolled her eyes. She might have given him too much credit on the maturing thing.

Luke and Sean reached their table, and she realized that she had watched them walk through the whole restaurant. God, she was such a hypocrite. Her only defense was that she didn't have her tongue hanging out, and she'd never been dumb enough to hop into bed with Luke.

Sean leaned down and kissed Rachel before taking the seat across from her in the middle chair. Shelly and Joe were already sitting on opposite sides of the table, so all the girls were on one side, which only left the seat directly on the other side of Elise open.

Great. This was supposed to be a relaxing night out with friends. She really didn't feel like being near King Flirt all evening.

It wasn't that she thought she was some irresistible beauty. In fact, he probably didn't even remember her. It was just that the Luke she remembered flirted with everyone who had a vagina.

Case in point, Luke walked over to Shelly and kissed her on the cheek. "Hey, gorgeous. How's my baby doing?"

Everybody laughed, even Joe. Elise snorted.

"You wish, Luke," Joe said.

Then, Luke kissed Rachel on the cheek. "Hey, beautiful. When are you going to leave that loser over there and marry me instead?"

"Never," Rachel told him with a grin on her face. "But I'll keep you in mind for when he kicks the bucket."

"Hey!" Sean exclaimed. But he was laughing, too. "I'm never dying, woman. You're stuck with me forever."

Luke went around to his side of the table and sat down across from Elise.

Sean pointed to her as Elise held out her hand to shake. "Luke, I don't know if you remember—"

"Elise Phillips," Luke said as he met her eyes. Taking her hand, he kissed the back of it, his trademark cocky smile on his face. "Of course I remember her. How could I forget?"

Like she said, flirt.

♡

Luke Long watched as Elise rolled her eyes, cupping the back of her hand where he'd kissed it, and he chuckled. He remembered that, back in college, it had always been easy to get a rise out of her, and it seemed things hadn't changed very much.

He knew she thought he was a dog, but it wasn't his fault that he liked sex and that women liked him. It wasn't as if he forced ladies to sleep with him. In fact, he usually waited for them to proposition him, and Elise probably wouldn't believe it, but he had said no a time or two.

But *she* had never been one of those girls. She'd never hit on him, and out of respect for his friendship with Sean, he'd never hit on her. Even though he knew she found him attractive. He'd seen the way she stared at him when he walked in the door today although she tried to hide it.

He always thought that one of the reasons she looked down on him so much was because there was unmistakable chemistry between them, and she hated it. While most girls had liked him back in college because he was a jock who played hockey, that hadn't seemed to impress Elise. This had only made him want to goad her more. Maybe it was the ten-year-old boy in him.

He could acknowledge that he might go a little overboard on the flirting, but flirting was fun, and he might as well drive Elise nuts since he couldn't sleep with her. Because, unlike her, he could admit he had wanted to—and apparently, still did.

She was pretty but not exceptionally beautiful, yet there was something about her. She was taller than most women, which he always liked since he was tall himself, and she was thin but not skinny. She had curves in all the right places, and she'd even filled out significantly more since college. She wasn't too big or too small. Like in *Goldilocks and the Three Bears*, she was *just* right. She had long dark blonde hair and large green doe-eyes. And big red lips that the guys in college had labeled DSL—dick-sucking lips.

He snickered, just thinking about it, and Elise narrowed her eyes at him.

Ha.

If she knew what he had been reminiscing about, she'd probably deck him. It was a good thing he wasn't going to tell her.

No, he wasn't going to say anything, and he'd do his best not to torture her tonight. He knew from Sean that she'd recently found out about her father's cancer, and she was busy moving and starting a new job. While Luke liked to provoke her, he'd like to think he wasn't a total asshole.

Yep, tonight was going to be nothing more than just a bunch of friends hanging out.

ABOUT THE AUTHOR

R.L. Kenderson is two best friends writing under one name.

Renae has always loved reading, and in third grade, she wrote her first poem where she learned she might have a knack for this writing thing. Lara remembers sneaking her grandmother's Harlequin novels when she was probably too young to be reading them, and since then, she knew she wanted to write her own.

When they met in college, they bonded over their love of reading and the TV show *Charmed*. What really spiced up their friendship was when Lara introduced Renae to romance novels. When they discovered their first vampire romance, they knew there would always be a special place in their hearts for paranormal romance. After being unable to find certain storylines and characteristics they wanted to read about in the hundreds of books they consumed, they decided to write their own.

One lives in the Minneapolis-St. Paul area and the other in the Kansas City area where they both work in the medical field during the day and a sexy author by night. They communicate through phone, email, and whole lot of messaging.

You can find them at http://www.rlkenderson.com, Facebook, Instagram, TikTok, and Goodreads. Join their reader group! Or you can email them at rlkenderson@rlkenderson .com, or sign up for their newsletter. They always love hearing from their readers.